A MOVEABLE FEAST

A BELOW STAIRS MYSTERY NOVELLA

JENNIFER ASHLEY

JA / AG PUBLISHING

CHAPTER 1

London 1884

On Saturday morning, the day before Easter, Mrs. Bywater, the mistress of the house, sailed into my kitchen in a rather somber gray frock and announced that I would be cooking Easter dinner at the home of her friend, Lady Babcock, in Portman Square.

In dismay, I yanked my hands from the bread dough I'd been kneading. Pots, pans, and crockery surrounded me on the table and the dresser, all in fullest use. Stewed mushrooms and beef stock bubbled on the stove, and the oven emitted scents of a rhubarb tart nearing completion.

What? I wanted to shriek.

I'd begun my labors on the Easter meal days ago. I had a large ham hock brined, ready for the oven tomorrow, plus a half dozen small fowl as well as a shank of mutton, all in their own stages of preparation. I'd stocked plenty of greens and vegetables to be cut and cooked at the last minute and had already made a start on the desserts. A cake with a roasted strawberry filling awaited fresh cream, and additional strawberries, along with other baked pastries, were in the larder.

My assistant, Tess, had spent hours chopping onions and celery into separate bowls for seasoning the meats and adding body to the vegetable dishes.

Mr. Davis, the butler, and I had gone over the wines both for the sauces and for serving at table, to pair just right with what I cooked.

In short, we had everything primed and organized so that I could finish the meal as efficiently as possible the next day. It would be ready for the family and staff members the moment they returned from the Easter service at the chapel around the corner.

And now the mistress calmly stood before me, ordering me to abandon it all and go cook in another woman's kitchen, without so much as a by-your-leave.

"I beg your pardon?" I finally managed to say.

My outrage must have shown, no matter how hard I tried to restrain myself, because Mrs. Bywater blinked.

"It should not be too much trouble, should it?" she asked. "Lady Babcock's cook is unwell, and her ladyship is hosting a large Easter dinner. She is at her wits' end. I had the thought: We could join Lord and Lady Babcock's dinner party and lend her our Mrs. Holloway. Why not? Lady Babcock readily agreed. You can cook a meal in another kitchen as well as this one, I'm certain. You are quite skilled."

She tacked on the flattery, which did not soften the blow. I imagined Mrs. Bywater pushing Lady Babcock into this decision as much as she was pushing me.

"It is not that simple, madam," I said stiffly. "Everything is at the ready. Do you mean for us to abandon this entire meal?" I waved at the food laid out around me. "Is that not a waste?"

Mrs. Bywater, the frugal soul, couldn't abide any sort of wastage—of money, time, or foodstuffs. She constantly reminded me of this.

"Not at all," was her brisk reply. "You will pack up everything and bring it with you."

I would, would I? My ire rose. Many of the dishes would not survive a move any farther than the upstairs dining room.

"Even if I could do such a thing, all this will not be enough if her ladyship is hosting a large dinner," I pointed out. "How many are attending?"

Mrs. Bywater shrugged. "Ten? Perhaps twenty, with our party joining? Lady Babcock's housekeeper will tell you when we arrive."

Tess listened to all this with her brown eyes wide, freckles standing out on her paling face. Her lips were parted, but fortunately she did not express her alarm out loud.

I barely contained my own. "There is a vast difference between cooking for ten and cooking for twenty, madam. Portions must be known, with extra planned in case there are hearty diners. It cannot be done. Her ladyship will simply have to hire out the meal or cancel it."

Mrs. Bywater's hazel eyes held impatience. "I fail to understand why you are creating such difficulties. Lady Babcock's cook will have already brought in the supplies for the meal, which, combined with ours, will be more than plenty. I have already promised Lady Babcock, so put these things together and come along. I've hired a cart to take you and all your dishes over, but we must make a start. Lady Babcock's housekeeper will arrange a place for you to sleep the night so you can begin cooking at the earliest possible hour in the morning."

I nearly gave my notice then and there. Tess, her knife poised over the endless stalks of celery, obviously feared I would do just that. If I walked off in anger, then *she* would be left with a half-cooked Easter dinner and a furious Mrs. Bywater.

For Tess's sake, I cooled my anger the best I could. Mrs. Bywater was correct that I could fix a fine meal to please her ladyship, even in the most difficult of circumstances. I reasoned that, like me, Lady Babcock's cook and housekeeper had already stocked the kitchen and been busy with preparations.

While Mrs. Bywater's faith in my skill was not misplaced, I did not fancy the mountain of extra work she'd abruptly piled upon Tess and me.

Also, she might have asked me beforehand instead of rashly promising my labor to her ladyship without my knowledge. Mrs. Bywater was ever in awe of a title, and no doubt she'd wanted to ingratiate herself with Lady Babcock, second wife of a widowed marquess.

I released a heavy sigh, conveying that anything I did henceforth was under duress. "I suppose we can salvage some of our foodstuffs. Tess and I will load the cart and take ourselves to her ladyship's kitchen. The kitchen staff do know we are arriving?"

"Not Tess," Mrs. Bywater stopped me by saying. "Only

you. Though of course Tess must help you carry things up to the road."

I let my hands fall to my sides, my anger renewed. "I must have Tess," I told her firmly. "Or else I shall not go."

Mrs. Bywater lifted her chin. "You are not to tell me what you shall or shall not do, Mrs. Holloway. Tess will be one too many in Lady Babcock's kitchen, and she will be needed here."

Tess sidled backward during this last exchange, as though ready to flee the house and return to her former existence of thieving for survival. I wanted to reassure her that all would be well, but I dared not look away from Mrs. Bywater.

"If I am to cook a large meal in an unknown kitchen, I cannot do it without Tess's help," I stated. "It is impossible. If there is a worry about where she will sleep, she can either bunk with me or return here for the night and set off again first thing in the morning."

Mrs. Bywater was a stubborn woman, used to having her way by means of bullying everyone with her nonstop chatter and the assumption that she'd already won. That she'd met her match for stubbornness in me was a constant annoyance to her.

I'd learned long ago to stand up for myself against those who considered me far beneath them. I might have been born in a London backstreet, but I had skills the higher-born needed, and they knew it. I was as much an aristocrat in my world as Lady Babcock was in hers.

I watched Mrs. Bywater debate which was the lesser evil—me bringing along my assistant or she having to tell Lady Babcock that her offered cook had refused to help. I might be sacked for my insolence, but I thought my agency would understand my plight.

Mrs. Bywater's mouth tightened as she made her choice. "Very well. Bring Tess along. I will leave it to you to make arrangements for her accommodation and wash my hands of the matter. If they do not want her there, it is nothing to do with me."

I nodded, pretending to be grateful. "Of course. We will begin packing at once."

Mrs. Bywater did not return my nod. "See that you do," she said coldly, and marched out of the kitchen, her heels clicking on the slate tiles as she stormed down the passageway toward the backstairs.

Once she was gone, Tess dropped her knife with a clatter and came around the table to me. "Mrs. H, what are we going to do?"

I wanted to sink to my chair, bury my face in my hands, and perhaps weep a bit, but I retained my composure. "Exactly what I said. We will gather our dishes and make our way to Portman Square."

"Won't all the things we made be ruined?"

"Possibly." I squared my shoulders. "We'll just have to do our best."

"You was going to save a bit back for Mr. McAdam," Tess reminded me.

I did remember this fact, ever so painfully. We'd known we could not be together for Easter dinner, it being a workday for me, but Daniel had promised to visit my kitchen later for a portion of the feast.

Scraps and leftovers only, of course. I'd never steal

foodstuffs from my employers to feed my beau, no matter how tempted I was.

Before I could answer Tess, Mr. Davis strode into the kitchen, his slim frame animated, his hairpiece slipping from the bald spot atop his head.

"Mrs. Holloway, that bloody woman has just told me to pack up all the bottles we've chosen and send them off with you," he raged. "She cannot mean to cart off all my wine."

"I am afraid she does, Mr. Davis." I did not want to deal with his fury, no matter how justified, as I was having enough trouble with my own. "It is our duty to comply, whether we like it or not."

Mr. Davis stared at me, as though surprised I wasn't waving my knife and declaring a mutiny. I gazed steadily back at him until he calmed a fraction.

"The master will hear of this," Mr. Davis said darkly.

Mr. Davis did not mean Mrs. Bywater's husband, who I wagered didn't fancy spending his Easter in the home of a stuffy marquess any more than we did. He referred to Lord Rankin, Mr. Bywater's nephew-in-law, who held the actual lease on the London house—he lived in seclusion in Surrey, allowing Mrs. Bywater to play lady of the manor in his Mount Street home.

Lord Rankin paid the salaries of all the staff and also the wine merchants' bills. If Lord Rankin objected to Mrs. Bywater giving away half the carefully selected wine cellar, *she'd* be accountable, not Mr. Davis or me.

"I will return what I do not use," I offered.

Mr. Davis threw up his hands. "It will not matter. Once the bottles are opened and exposed to air, they will be useless if not drunk immediately. You might as well pour them into the cistern."

He stalked away after this pronouncement, in high dudgeon.

Mr. Davis exaggerated, though only slightly. I'd tote the half-empty bottles home, and he and Mrs. Redfern could enjoy their contents during their late-night chats in the housekeeper's parlor.

For now, Tess and I had much work to do.

The cakes and pastries would fare the best, if we were careful. We wrapped them in clean cheesecloth and laid them into small crates, ensuring that the heaviest cakes were on the bottom. I had to assume the Portman Square kitchen would have cream I could whip and other fresh things I couldn't tote. I put the strawberries into another crate along with root vegetables and fruits I would prepare tomorrow. Their staff should have gotten in greens and other produce, I reasoned, though not any I had picked over.

The ham, in its roasting pan, went into another small crate that I covered with paper and cheesecloth, as did the mutton shank and the quail, ready to be dressed. The stock I'd been reducing for my sauce would have to remain. I'd inspect the other kitchen's stocks and broths once I got there and adjust them to my taste.

I briefly considered bringing my own knives, as a cook grows as accustomed to them as she does her own hands, but declined. I didn't want to risk one getting lost in the commotion or an unskilled undercook ruining a blade.

Mr. Davis unbent enough to lay the bottles of wine into a few more boxes, cushioning them with straw. He carried these upstairs himself and set them into the waiting cart, admonishing the driver, who listened with a disagreeable frown, not to jolt them in any way.

Tess and Mr. Davis helped me lug out the rest of the crates, fitting them carefully into the cart. Once we were finished, and Tess had climbed up to ride with the driver, I realized there was no room for me.

"I can walk, Mrs. H.," Tess declared, preparing to descend.

"No, indeed." Tess was slim enough to perch on the small space on the driver's seat, but my plump body would be too tight a fit. "It is a fine day for a stroll. Just mind that no one squashes the goods if you begin to unload before I reach the house."

The driver, who apparently concluded we'd lingered long enough, started the large horse. Tess, clearly unhappy, gazed back at me as they rolled away.

Mr. Davis had already retreated to sulk, so I descended one final time to the kitchen, folded a clean apron into a basket to which I added a few sealed pots of spices, and donned my coat and hat.

The most direct route to Portman Square was west along Mount Street to Park Street—one over from the sumptuous Park Lane—and then straight north until I reached the square.

I had just crossed Oxford Street when a delivery van pulled by a large draft horse rolled to a halt beside me. "Mrs. Holloway," came its driver's cheerful call. "Can I be of assistance? I can save your feet, if nothing else."

aniel McAdam, his tall son James beside him, grinned cheerfully down at me, never minding other carts and wagons who now had to pull around him.

My gladness in seeing Daniel unnerved me a bit. We'd grown more tender with each other of late, but I was a cook, while he worked in some capacity for the police when he was not driving a delivery vehicle. Ours was not the romance of legends, and my heart had no business leaping high every time I beheld the man.

I strove to sound offhand. "I have not far to go now, so it is no matter. Thank you for the offer, of course."

Daniel's sunny smile barely dimmed. "Where are you heading on this fine Saturday afternoon? The markets are in the other direction."

I adjusted the heavy basket on my arm. "Mrs. Bywater ordered me to cook Easter dinner at the home of her friend in Portman Square. Not an hour ago, this was."

At last, I'd managed to astonish him. Daniel handed

the reins to James, who was equally astonished, and scrambled down.

"Portman Square?" Daniel asked me sharply.

I eyed him in trepidation. "Please do not tell me you are stalking a horrible criminal in Portman Square and that I, Tess, and the guests will be in grave danger there."

"No, no." Daniel said this too quickly for my taste. "I am surprised, is all. What has happened?"

I hardly had time to stand in the street and chat, but this was Daniel. He soon had the entire story out of me.

"Inconsiderate of her," Daniel agreed when I finished. "Mrs. Bywater is the sort of woman who doesn't quite believe other people are human, isn't she? They exist as characters in her personal drama, with no lives of their own when they have left the stage."

I hadn't thought of it like that, but Daniel's description was apt. "In any case, I must be off. Tess went ahead with the supplies, and I do not want the kitchen staff browbeating her. Who knows if they were told she was coming with me?"

"Tess is a resilient young woman," Daniel reminded me. "You have given her much confidence. I agree with Mrs. Bywater in one respect—you will do a fine job of it, even rushed in a strange kitchen with unfamiliar staff."

"Very kind," I said with irritation. "I'd rather not have the bother, thank you very much."

Instead of being contrite, Daniel continued cheerily, "One day, you'll be able to put your feet up for good. I promise."

My heart fluttered, and I admonished it. Did Daniel

mean he'd accomplish this scenario on my behalf? Or only that it was inevitable?

"That day seems very far away," I replied grumpily. "I'll likely be too old and doddering to walk at all, by that time."

"Poor Kat." I read sympathy in Daniel, even as he laughed at me. "Be resolute until Monday, and then I will give you and Grace a grand afternoon out."

"I apologize for my temper," I said in sudden remorse. "I was caught by surprise by my mistress's impulsiveness. This means I cannot promise you a good meal if you stop to chat Sunday night. Though I'd be happy to see you, in any case."

As we stood on the street, Daniel did not try to press my hand, or heaven forbid, kiss me, but he leaned close and spoke in a low voice. "I will be happy to see you at any time."

My heart fluttered again, but I made myself restrict our farewell to a friendly nod. "I look forward to it. Now, I must get on. Keep well, James," I called up to the young man.

"And you, Mrs. H.," James said good-naturedly. "I'll look after this one." He pointed a gloved finger at his father.

Daniel's smile turned wry. He tipped his hat to me, scrambled up to the driver's seat, and saluted me once more before he took the reins and chirruped to the horse.

I hid my glumness as the delivery van ambled away, unhappy I had to say goodbye to the two who'd become very close to me and face a daunting task.

I firmed my resolve and trudged the final block to Portman Square.

————

WHAT AWAITED me was worse than I'd feared.

The house, which stood on the north side of the square, two doors down from Upper Berkley Street, did have a fairly well-appointed kitchen. A stove of a later model than mine gleamed on a bed of tiles, its stovepipe fixed into an old chimney behind it.

Bright copper pots and cooking utensils dangled from racks, the kitchen table was wide and ample, and a carved Welsh dresser loaded with crockery stood against a wall. The flagstone floor had been recently scrubbed, and the whitewashed walls brought a refreshing lightness to the room.

The staff, on the other hand, were next to hopeless. Tess stood among them, minus her hat and coat, scowling her most fearsome scowl. A plump, middle-aged woman in a brown frock, whom I took to be the housekeeper, stood near the dresser regarding Tess, me, and the crates we'd brought in vexation.

"What am I meant to do with this lot?" she demanded.

I remained as unruffled as I could while I hung up my coat and hat and unrolled my apron. "We will sort out the food and add it to what has already been prepared," I said as calmly as I could. "It is not ideal, but I'm certain that between us, we can fix a fine meal for the upstairs, with a nice one for ourselves afterward."

One of the two kitchen maids perked up at my last

utterance, but the second one studied me with intense dislike.

"Cook's already got in her own supplies," the housekeeper said sourly. "Mrs. Morgan won't be wanting other things cluttering up her kitchen."

From what I could see, Mrs. Morgan hadn't brought much into her kitchen at all. One pot simmered on the stove, emitting a scent of old beef, but no other cooking scents pervaded the air. It was apparent that when the cook had fallen ill, the other staff hadn't stepped in to take up the slack.

"I am sorry to hear she is doing poorly," I stated. "Mrs. Morgan must be wretched, not being able to bustle about her own kitchen on this important occasion."

"Aye, she's in a bad way." The housekeeper nodded, though she did not appear to have much sympathy for her colleague. "Had stomachache all day Thursday, soldiered through part of the day yesterday, and couldn't heave herself from the bed this morning."

"Poor soul," I said. "I hope she is soon better. I am Mrs. Holloway, and your mistress has brought me in to finish the meal. This is Tess Parsons, my assistant. She is quite skilled and will help me but stay out of your way."

I ceased speaking, waiting for them to introduce themselves, but all three simply stared at me, the housekeeper and one maid glowering, the younger kitchen maid regarding me in open curiosity.

I turned to the more interested maid, who had dark hair and eyes and a rather square, plain face. "What is your name, my dear?"

"I'm Mary," she answered readily. "This is Jane." She

jabbed a thumb at the maid beside her. Jane had an oval face, lighter brown hair, and blue eyes. Her churlish expression marred the prettiness she otherwise possessed.

"I can speak for meself," Jane snapped. "How d'ya do, I'm sure."

"Keep a civil tongue, Jane," the housekeeper admonished. "I'm Mrs. Seabrook, if we must make introductions as though we are at tea. I'll not take orders from you, Mrs. Cook."

"I'd not expect you to." I strove to keep my tone even. "If you will show me the larder, I can make a start."

"I've better things to do than take you around the downstairs," Mrs. Seabrook said sharply. "Jane will do that. Is that wine in them crates?" She moved to one whose lid Tess had loosened and peeked into it. "You'd better save back a few bottles for the footmen, or you'll get nothing accomplished. Give them to Armitage. He's butler." Mrs. Seabrook frowned as Tess and I stared at her. "Come on then, Mrs. Cook. There's much to do."

With that, she turned on her heel and marched out of the room, Mary watching her go with uncertainty.

I made myself turn to the table. I'd immerse myself in cooking—*with* all the wine I'd brought—and we'd leave this house tomorrow afternoon. There was no need for me to befriend a bad-tempered housekeeper.

"Now then, Jane," I said briskly. "Let us look at the larder."

"I don't take orders from ya, neither," Jane informed me. "I work for Mrs. Morgan. Old Bat Seabrook don't frighten me, and neither do you."

Tess darted forward. "Look 'ere, you—"

I put myself between the two young women. "I'm certain I can find my way on my own. Carry on with what you were doing." Which didn't seem to be much of anything, from the lack of foodstuffs on the table.

I sent Tess a soothing glance and departed the kitchen, turning left in the passageway to where the larder was most likely to be. Most servants' areas in this part of London were laid out in a similar fashion, and I quickly found the linen cupboard, laundry room, and larder.

Pattering footsteps sounded behind me, and Mary caught up to me on the larder's threshold.

"Don't mind Jane," she said apologetically. "She's all sourness at the best of times. What can I show you, Mrs. Holloway?"

"Thank you, Mary." I softened my tone, grateful for one friendly voice. "I need to see all the produce you have stocked, plus we'll need plenty of cream and the best fresh herbs. Where are her spice boxes?"

"I don't know about any of that." Mary stood in the middle of the larder, regarding the jumble of crates and the shelves as though she'd never seen them before. "Mrs. Morgan don't let me in here much. There's some flour, there." She pointed to a large sack that had leaked to the stones, staining them white. "We'll need that for the bread, won't we?"

I was already rooting around the shelves, uncovering bags of such dried foodstuffs as rice and macaroni, but no produce at all. A wooden box marked *Cheese* held nothing but moldy bits that needed to be discarded. I did discover a few pots of spices, but they must have been ancient, because they barely had any odor. I was grateful I'd remembered to bring some of my own.

I turned to Mary, who had her hands wrapped nervously in her apron. "Why won't Mrs. Morgan allow you into the larder? What exactly do you do in the kitchen?"

"I sort things and stir what Mrs. Morgan tells me to stir," Mary said. "Mostly I scrub what dishes she's done with."

"Don't you have a scullery maid for that?" I asked in surprise. Lord Babcock was a marquess, who ought to have a servant for every conceivable task under the sun.

"I *were* a scullery maid. But Mrs. Morgan said she needed more hands, so I was brought into the kitchen. I still have to do the scullery work. Jane is more of the under-cook. Mrs. Morgan lets her chop the vegetables. She won't let *me* near a knife, except to wash it."

"I see." I was glad I'd stood up to Mrs. Bywater and brought Tess along. "Do you have any idea where Mrs. Morgan keeps her vegetables? In the kitchen itself?" The larder was a much better place for storage, as it was generally always cool, free of drafts, and not heated by the stove, but I'd already seen that this kitchen was not very efficient.

"Don't know." Mary looked troubled. "Sorry, Missus. Mrs. Morgan don't show us much, only expects us to do what we're told."

No wonder Jane wore a perpetual scowl while Mary existed in a state of bewilderment.

"It is no matter, Mary," I said. "We'll muddle along." I'd found nothing in the larder I wanted to use and gestured her out. "Let us see what she's begun in the kitchen for tomorrow's dinner."

"Not much, I think." Mary trotted after me, still trying to be helpful. "Mrs. Morgan's been so very ill."

"Nothing contagious, I hope," I said as though I wasn't worried, but truth to tell, I was. What had laid the cook so low, so quickly?

"Mrs. Seabrook says no," Mary said. "Just an ailment. Her ladyship has been nursing her ever so kindly."

"Huh." Jane heard her as we entered the kitchen. "Her ladyship is likely trying to pry the old besom out of bed. I'm surprised her ladyship let you come at all, Mrs. Holloway. She don't like those she don't know."

"You shouldn't talk about the mistress like that." Mary darted a glance behind her as though someone would overhear and report directly to Lady Babcock. And possibly, they would. Servants in unhappy situations sometimes strove to better their lot by telling tales on others.

Tess, who'd put herself on the opposite side of the table from Jane, frowned in agreement with Mary. Tess always had plenty to say about the family she worked for, but I had the feeling she'd be contrary to anything Jane uttered.

"I'm certain her ladyship is doing all she can," I said firmly. "Where are the vegetables, Jane? I want to sort what I need for tomorrow."

"Some tatties over there." Jane pointed with the tip of a knife to a crate in the corner. "Some cabbages too, but they don't look nice."

"I see." I bit back sharper words. "What has Mrs.

Morgan planned for the meat? Ham? Roast lamb? Capons for one of the courses?"

"She hadn't gone to the butcher's afore she fell sick," Jane informed me. "So, I don't know, do I?"

"Well, what were you planning to give the upstairs for Easter dinner?" I demanded. "Boiled rice and old cabbage?"

"Don't ask me, missus," Jane returned. "I'm a kitchen maid. If you don't need me help, then I'm off." She started to untie her apron.

"No, you will stay right here." The time for friendly cajoling had passed. "Fortunately, I brought plenty of my own foodstuffs. You will help Tess sort it, and I will go to the markets and find what I can, though there won't be much left by now."

Jane glared at me defiantly, but after a time under my stern gaze, she took her hand from her apron ties. "Yes, missus," she said sullenly.

"Mrs. Morgan went to the market yesterday morning," Mary offered, her voice faint. "But I don't know what she did with the things."

Tess shook her head at me. I guessed she'd had a poke about the kitchen in my absence and found nothing of use.

I peered into the back of the room. "Tess, if that is broth on the stove, will you make certain it's hot? I will take a cup upstairs to Mrs. Morgan and ask her. I'm certain she'll not want his lordship's dinner to be an absolute disaster."

The quirk of Jane's lips hinted she wouldn't mind a disaster and possibly would find it diverting, but I could not risk my reputation in such a manner. Also, I had enough respect for those I fed to not want them suffering through a terrible meal.

Tess moved the stockpot to another burner and checked the firebox beneath, tossing in a small piece of wood. She stirred the stock, which soon began to steam.

I fetched a bowl from the dresser, which I was happy to find clean. Mary might not know her way around a kitchen, but it was clear she did her scrubbing job well.

I found a ladle and filled the bowl with the hot broth and set it on a plate, laying this on a tray with a spoon. It would have been nice to add a heel of fresh bread or a cup of tea, but neither of those were at the ready.

"Carry on with the sorting," I told Tess and Jane. "Have Mary help with what she can. I will take this up to the cook, and then I'm off to the shops."

Mary nodded readily, but the other two only watched me go unhappily.

I carried the tray down the hall to the backstairs. As I passed what I'd deduced was the door to the butler's pantry, a small but plump and red-faced man in a black tailcoat popped from it.

"You the new cook?" he demanded in a thick east London accent.

"I am Mrs. Holloway," I said, ignoring his bad manners. "You are Armitage?"

"I am." He pointed his finger at me. "You won't touch any of me wines. A cook what wants wine for her sauces is only looking to have a go at the bottle herself, am I right?"

By the redness of his face and the broken veins on his

nose, I would guess that Mr. Armitage "had a go" fairly often himself.

"That is not entirely true, Mr. Armitage. Now, if you will excuse me."

I turned my back on him to mount the staircase. I felt him watch me go, but at least he didn't say anything further.

I hadn't assured him I'd brought my own bottles, because I didn't want him absconding with them while I was away from the kitchen. Mrs. Seabrook's order that I save some to bribe the footmen told me what sort of household this was. Even if the footmen preferred a good ale to a fancy wine, they could make a few quid selling the bottles on.

Lady Babcock truly needed to review her staff and pay attention to what went on below stairs. Mrs. Bywater was apt to give us too much attention, but I decided now it might be the lesser of the evils.

I then wondered *why* Lady Babcock didn't bother herself. Most aristocratic women were sticklers about their household running smoothly, because a badly run one was talked about and reflected poorly on them. I supposed she might have been brought up to leave every-thing to the housekeeper and butler, but that only worked if the senior staff were competent. Even the most honest domestics would soon take advantage of a slack mistress, once they'd learned they could.

I reached the main floor then continued to the upper ones, balancing the tray as I climbed the steep staircase. I hadn't asked where Mrs. Morgan's bedroom was, but most of the staff in townhouses slept at the top, so there I headed.

This house had four floors below the attic, and I was puffing by the time I reached the top story, the tray growing heavy.

The attic held a narrow hallway, which was obviously a recent addition, leading past the servants' bedrooms. In earlier centuries, the female staff usually slept together in one large chamber, the male staff in another, often three and more to a bed. Senior servants—cooks, house-keepers, butlers, and valets—could have their own cubbyhole somewhere or they might bunk in with the others.

At some point in my lifetime, employers decided that servants should be separated from one another and so built partition walls in the attics with doors to close off the rooms. Whether that was out of kindness or fear that we'd cause more trouble lumped together, I wasn't certain.

Mrs. Morgan had a room rather like mine, small with whitewashed walls that contained a bed, a night table, a washstand with pitcher and bowl, and a small bureau. I'd added a few things to my chamber over the years, such as a framed picture of flowers Joanna had given me and trinkets I'd purchased here and there, as well as several secondhand books. Mrs. Morgan had nothing like that in view.

She lay on the bed, her face as gray as her hair, obviously so miserable that my testiness evaporated.

"Mrs. Morgan?" I spoke in a gentle voice. "Do not be alarmed. I am Mrs. Holloway, who will be cooking in your stead. I've brought you a bit of broth, which will give you strength."

Mrs. Morgan heaved a rattling breath. She was neither startled nor angered by my presence, and she did not try to sit up. "Glad you've come," she said wearily.

I set the tray on the dresser and used my handkerchief to take up the hot bowl of broth and carry it to her. I would likely have to spoon-feed her, but I didn't mind helping the poor thing.

Before I could begin, the door opened behind me. "Now then, Mrs. Morgan," a soft voice proclaimed. "I've brought you another cup of tea—oh."

I turned to see a small-statured woman, with a face that showed she'd been a stunning woman in her youth and was pretty still in middle age. Her dark hair, which bore only a few threads of gray, was coiled and curled with the vigor of the latest fashions. She wore a gown so ruffled and frilled I feared she'd tear it simply walking through the corridor outside.

The lady regarded me with ingenuous blue eyes that held faint puzzlement, and I curtsied the best I could while balancing the full bowl of broth.

"Ah." Mrs. Bywater, who entered behind her, promptly took command of the situation. "This is *my* cook, your ladyship. I told you she'd come along and save you." She skewered me with her cool stare. "I suppose you are here to nurse Mrs. Morgan, but there is no need. We are taking great care of her, aren't we?" She added this in a nursery-maid tone to Mrs. Morgan, who regarded her limply.

Lady Babcock seemed in no way aggrieved that Mrs. Bywater was so obviously currying favor with her. "I am so pleased you came," she said to me, her voice rather childlike. "You can return to your kitchen. Your mistress and I have charge of Mrs. Morgan now."

Lady Babcock did not wear the expression of someone impatient with another's illness, so I decided Mary had the right of her motives, not Jane.

"Make sure she takes all the broth," I said, setting the bowl on the night table. "It will do her much good."

Mrs. Bywater pointedly held the door open for me. "Off you go then, Mrs. Holloway."

I still needed to know how the kitchen was supplied, but Mrs. Morgan did not seem up to discussing her inventory with me. I'd have to go to the markets and buy whatever I needed, telling the grocers to put the purchases on Lord Babcock's account.

A shaky but surprisingly strong hand caught my wrist. I looked down to see Mrs. Morgan gazing up at me imploringly. "Stay," she whispered.

CHAPTER 3

$\mathcal{M}$rs. Morgan's eyes were wide—with fear? Of whom? Lady Babcock? Or Mrs. Bywater, who could be trying on the best of days?

Whatever the cause, I could not in good conscience leave her here alone. "I will need to feed her the broth," I said to the two women who obviously waited for me to go.

Mrs. Morgan regarded me gratefully as I sat down on the edge of her bed and took up the spoon.

Lady Babcock stared at me as though she had no idea how to respond, while Mrs. Bywater frowned, used to my impertinence.

As I appeared to have planted myself firmly at Mrs. Morgan's side, Lady Babcock set the cup of tea on top of the bureau and retreated to the open doorway. "You'll be better in no time," she told Mrs. Morgan with the optimism of those in a sickroom. "And back in your kitchen soon. Won't you?"

Mrs. Morgan concentrated on the spoon I lifted to her

lips and didn't answer. Mrs. Bywater sent her a disapproving gaze, as though she expected Mrs. Morgan to leap from her bed, curtsey, and promise to hurry down and cook the Easter meal.

The two ladies at last withdrew, but I noted they left the door ajar. I could not rise to close it, as Mrs. Morgan was hungrily drinking broth from my spoon. I wondered if anyone in this house had offered the woman anything more substantial than tea.

When at last Mrs. Morgan breathed a little easier, I set aside the broth, rose and closed the door, fetching the tea on my way back to the bed.

"You're a good woman," Mrs. Morgan croaked at me in a half whisper. "Even if ya is too young."

"I assure you, I can provide his lordship a decent meal for Easter," I said. "You worry about nothing. I suppose you've put plenty by for the task?"

I didn't like to trouble her about the food when she was so wretched, but I needed to begin somewhere.

"Have a care while you're in this house," was her answer.

Curiosity plucked at me. "Why do you say that?" Mrs. Seabrook was unfriendly and the butler a drunkard, but I'd dealt with such things before.

Mrs. Morgan snaked her fingers around my wrist once again and pulled me closer.

"Her ladyship ain't wanted," she whispered, her breath unpleasant. "No one can stick her."

"We can't always love those we work for," I said, trying to soothe her. "Else none of us would find a position."

"Seabrook bows and scrapes to her, but she don't like

her. Nor do the rest of the 'ouse. Used to be nobody, did her ladyship. A tart by all accounts. Watch out for her."

I stared at Mrs. Morgan in perplexity.

I'd met aging courtesans before, who used powder and other artifices to hide their wrinkles, but there wasn't a trace of any of this on Lady Babcock's face. Also, those women had maintained their regal arrogance, confident in their ability to entice princes and foreign kings, even if those days had passed.

Lady Babcock wore fashionable clothing, and her hair was a la mode, but in no way did she resemble a former courtesan. More a woman fading into middle age, trying to hold on to her youth by dressing smartly.

"Do you mean she is dangerous?" I asked, though I could not see how Lady Babcock could be.

Mrs. Morgan didn't answer. Her grip on me slackened, her head sank into the pillow, and in another moment, a snore issued from her mouth.

Stifling a sigh, I gathered up the bowl of broth. I could leave the tea for her, but by the time she woke, it would be stone cold. I'd have Tess or Mary check on her later and bring her a fresh cup.

The tea shouldn't go to waste, however. I was thirsty from my trek from Mount Street and my frustration with the kitchen staff, and the tea, which Mrs. Morgan hadn't touched and wasn't likely to, enticed me.

I lifted the cup and took a long swallow, then grimaced. The tea was far too bitter and strong. Either Lady Babcock had no idea how to brew up, or those in this household liked it muddy.

I poured the rest of the tea into the slop pail by the

washstand, piled the soiled crockery on the tray, and carried it out of the room, closing the door firmly behind me.

As I descended, I wondered if Mrs. Morgan's admonition for me to stay with her had been for fear of Lady Babcock or out of annoyance at both ladies' intrusion. In any case, Lady Babcock did not strike me as a woman who could engender terror in her servants. Her manner had been hesitant and lacking steel, but Mrs. Morgan's words had been adamant.

Watch out for her.

I'd once briefly worked for a frail, elderly, weak-voiced woman who couldn't rise from her bed and yet had kept the entire household firmly under her thumb. None dared make a move without approval from the lady's chamber. When the lady had finally died, her entire family had immediately scattered, as though in relief, and I'd returned to my agency to seek another post.

Perhaps Lady Babcock was of similar dominance, never raising her voice but controlling all aspects of those around her.

I returned to the kitchen, reasoning that I would not be in this house long enough to determine whether Lady Babcock was a quiet martinet or not.

Knowing I'd have to go to the markets myself, I deposited the used crockery at the sink, put away the tray, and took up my things, ready to hunt for produce and other necessities in Oxford Street.

"I won't be long," I promised, lifting my now-empty basket. Tess at least had been diligent about unpacking. "Start the mushrooms brewing, so we'll have a good, strong stock from them, and continue preparing the onions and leeks we brought."

"Don't you worry none, Mrs. Holloway," Tess assured me. "We'll manage until you're back."

"Why can't *you* go?" Jane demanded of Tess. "She's the cook. Shouldn't you be out drudging for the vittals while she lords it over us in the kitchen?"

Tess's scowl instantly returned.

"I can more quickly find the choicest greens and best fish," I said before Tess could speak. "My experience is better put to choosing the vegetables than chopping onions. Which I expect to be done by the time I return, Jane. If ensuring you do the job you are paid to is lording it over you, well then, so be it. We'll have a nice repast in the end for all our hard work. You'll see."

I wrenched open the door and scurried out under Jane's glare. She was a hard one, and resentful, but hopefully I could soften her a bit before I went home.

As I trudged along to Oxford Street, a wave of near despair washed over me. Why was I bothering to put together an Easter feast for a family who knew nothing of me, among kitchen staff who didn't want me there? I'd agreed under duress because of Mrs. Bywater, a woman who, after all, did not actually pay my salary. Lord Rankin did.

Why should I not turn around, fetch Tess, return home, and dare Mrs. Bywater to do anything about it? I doubted *Mr.* Bywater would let her sack me, and their niece, Lady Cynthia, would do everything in her power to keep me at the house, I was certain.

I halted near the door of my favorite greengrocers and

leaned against the brick wall, suddenly needing a rest. I concluded I was exhausted from all the work I'd done preparing the supper for the Bywaters and their few guests—which had included Mr. Thanos—and now I had to do this extra shopping and cooking for a mob. I had no stamina for it.

I took a moment of self-pity, which was unusual for me. But really, I had been much put upon, even for one of the servant classes.

I straightened up, drew a long breath, and entered the greengrocers.

As I'd suspected, he had little left, but as I was one of the man's best customers, he always kept something back in case I needed it. Thus, I was able to at least procure some decent greens and better potatoes than what waited for me in the Portman Square kitchen.

I thanked him profusely, directed him to charge the purchases to Lord Babcock, and departed to visit the fishmonger and butcher. Though my tiredness jumbled my thoughts a bit, I arranged for fresh sole to be delivered to the house as well as another ham, along with some oxtail and beef bones so I could make soup and aspic.

A deeper wave of lethargy swept over me as I finished the shopping and began the short walk back to Portman Square.

I halted in the middle of Portman Street amid people scurrying home to prepare for their own Easter celebration and fought a sudden need to lie down and sleep.

I forced my eyes to remain open, wondering what on earth was wrong with me. This was more than me feeling sorry for myself because I'd been suddenly overwhelmed with work. Was I ill? Had Mrs. Morgan been contagious after all?

Propping myself against the iron railings that surrounded the park in Portman Square, I went over my symptoms. I was seldom ill, but my ailments usually manifested in a scratchy throat and stuffy nose, with the occasional fever. I had none of these, my skin cool and damp rather than hot and dry.

Though tired, I seemed to be as robust as ever. I reasoned that even if Mrs. Morgan did carry an infectious illness, it wouldn't have gripped me so quickly.

However, there was no question about my sudden fatigue. It was most odd. The only time I'd felt like this was long ago, when I'd strained my wrist and a doctor had given me a bit of laudanum to ease the pain. I'd not liked the medicine and refused to take the rest of the dose he'd left with me.

Laudanum. The realization made me suck in a breath of cool air, which woke me a bit.

Where on earth had I taken laudanum?

The answer came to me at once. The tea. I'd had a swallow of Mrs. Morgan's tea after she'd fallen asleep, finding the taste strangely bitter.

Good heavens. Lady Babcock had dosed Mrs. Morgan's tea with laudanum.

Had she thought this might help the cook get well more swiftly? Possibly. Some believed that laudanum and opium were the best cure for any ailment. Perhaps this was Lady Babcock's usual remedy, and Mrs. Morgan had known full well what was in the tea Lady Babcock had carried into the room.

But then, Mrs. Morgan had eyed Lady Babcock in trepidation and begged me not to leave her.

Watch out for her.

Daniel had given me a sharp look when I'd mentioned Portman Square. He'd assured me he hadn't been on the trail of a criminal there, but he hadn't explained what had made him uneasy.

Was Lady Babcock a mad poisoner, with the police poised to arrest her the moment anyone in her household died?

I pushed myself from the railings with a laugh. What nonsense. If Lady Babcock were a poisoner, Daniel would have warned me outright.

Lady Babcock might simply have been trying to nurse her cook. The amount of laudanum I'd swallowed in the tea hadn't been enough to send me unconscious before I made it down the stairs. Even now, I could still walk and think, the drink slowing me only somewhat.

Still, I longed for a good nap, and cursed Lady Babcock for not bothering to mention that she'd laced the tea with an opiate. My own foolishness for drinking it.

Keeping close to the railings, in case I had to hold myself up again, I continued along the street and around the corner to Lord Babcock's townhome. I took the stairs down to the kitchen carefully, balancing myself against the rather slimy brick wall.

The kitchen bustled with activity, I was pleased to see. Both Tess and Jane were chopping things, and Mary busily washed pots and crockery in the scullery.

"I managed to get some vegetables." I set my basket on the table with exaggerated care then fumbled with the buttons of my coat, which fell to the floor before I could catch it. "Tess, please start on these onions. Jane, you will clean and chop the carrots. I need them in tiny bits, to make the sauce more robust."

Jane studied me with her usual scowl, but she didn't argue.

I tried to hang my coat on a hook, missed, and tried again, my fingers trembling.

"Whatever is the matter with you, Cook?" Mrs. Seabrook had swept into the kitchen and now stared hard at me.

"Nothing." I concentrated again on getting my coat onto the hook. Almost there.

"Good Lord." Mrs. Seabrook's glare seared me. "You're tipsy. Of all the things I've been saddled with in the last week, now the mistress's silly friend brought in a drunk cook. Her ladyship will hear of this."

So saying, Mrs. Seabrook marched from the kitchen, heels clattering on the slate floor as she made for the backstairs.

CHAPTER 4

I hurried after Mrs. Seabrook the best I could. My coat, which had fallen once more, remained in a heap on the floor.

"I am never drunk," I declared as I caught up to her. "I was foolish to go up to Mrs. Morgan, is all. I drank tea meant for her, which I believe had a drop of laudanum in it."

"Nonsense." Mrs. Seabrook turned on me. "None use laudanum in this house. Her ladyship has medicines from her doctor, but she'd not dispense them to the servants. There's naught wrong with Mrs. Morgan, in any case. She's malingering. She and her ladyship have been quarreling something fierce, probably over the menus. They don't see eye to eye. Mrs. Morgan decided to dodge cooking what she didn't want by pretending to fall sick. Her ladyship has been contrite ever since."

"No, no, Mrs. Morgan is quite ill," I insisted. "Could scarcely lift her head from her pillow. There was laudanum in the tea, I'm certain of it, but I will be fine in a trice. I shake off these things quite quickly."

Armitage had emerged from his butler's pantry as we argued. "Nay, she's tipsy all right," he said to Mrs. Seabrook. "I told her, cooks what use wine in their sauces only want a good tipple from the bottle."

"I am not drunk!" I shouted at the pair of them. "You can smell my breath, if you don't believe me."

Mrs. Seabrook and Armitage leaned to me, prepared to do just that. Armitage drew back immediately, his tone dropping to a mutter. "Well, some learn to hide it."

Mrs. Seabrook continued to eye me suspiciously. "I'll keep silent for now. You get back to the kitchen and produce that meal for tomorrow. If I find you nodding off over it, I'll send you away and tell your mistress to give you the sack. I mean it."

I drew myself up as much as my lingering stupor allowed. "I do not tipple, as I have stated. The meal will commence, Mrs. Seabrook. You look out for Mrs. Morgan and see her well again."

"Not my place." Mrs. Seabrook stuck her nose in the air and made for the housekeeper's parlor. "Get on with it, Cook."

"Yes, get on with it," Armitage echoed. "And cease shouting in the hallways. I have work to do."

I could smell *his* breath from where I stood, and the quantity of wine on it. No wonder he'd so quickly realized I had none on mine.

"If I am not subject to ridiculous accusations, I can commence with my own duties. Good day, Mr. Armitage."

Armitage grumbled something, retreated to the butler's pantry, and slammed its door. I heaved a sigh—I'd been doing much of that today—and returned to the kitchen.

All three young women paused to watch as I came in. My coat had been placed neatly on the coat rack, and I assumed Tess had hung it there for me. I felt a bit better already—my rage at Mrs. Seabrook and Armitage seemed to have helped clear the substance from my blood.

"I suggest we ignore further interruptions," I instructed. "We have much to accomplish. Jane, when you've done the carrots, I'll show you how to store the greens to keep them fresh for tomorrow."

As both maids bent over their tasks, I stepped to the sink in the scullery and seized the cup I'd taken from Mrs. Morgan's room before Mary could drop it into the sudsy water.

Mary regarded me with perplexity, but I hurried past her back to the kitchen, surreptitiously sliding the cup into a drawer in the dresser.

I moved to the table and began to sort what was in the basket, but my legs trembled, and I had to sit down quickly to do it.

SOMEHOW, we managed to finish our preparations that afternoon, Tess and I recreating what we'd done in my kitchen and carefully storing the pastries and tarts we'd brought with us.

I mixed bread dough and kneaded it, letting it rise for

baking in the morning, plus broke off a small piece to roll into buns for the kitchen staff's supper that night.

Apparently, a meal wasn't required for the household that evening, as his lordship and his son, Lord Alfred Charlton, had gone to their club. Lady Babcock was out with her stepdaughter, Lady Margaret, who was quite a beauty and would likely marry anyone she chose, according to Mary. Only the staff needed to be fed, and I knew I could prepare a good supper for us all.

As I worked on this and tomorrow's feast, I felt much better, the effects of the laudanum wearing off. I wasn't certain what I'd do with the unwashed cup I'd hidden, but it was evidence I hadn't muddled my head with drink.

Mary, who'd quickly grown comfortable with me and Tess, chattered away about Lord Babcock and his family. It was common knowledge that Lady Babcock was his lordship's second wife, and that the son and daughter of the household, both in their twenties, were children of the marquess and his first wife.

Lord Alfred was being groomed to step into the marquess's shoes whenever Lord Babcock popped off. Lady Margaret, as Mary had mentioned, was quite beautiful and had any number of suitors. Lady Margaret sometimes came down to the kitchen, sweet as you please, to ask for a dish to be made for tea with her friends, or to snatch a tidbit, as she'd been doing since she was a child.

Mary had no use at all for the second Lady Babcock. It seemed no one did, though she'd been Lord Babcock's wife for the past twenty years.

I did not condone gossiping in the kitchen, but I admit

I didn't stop Tess asking questions. Nor did I make myself not listen to the answers.

"Lord Alfred will likely toss her ladyship out on her ear when he inherits," Mary said with confidence. "Stands to reason. She ain't their mum, is she?"

"Is Lord Babcock likely to fall off his perch any time soon?" Tess asked with unfeigned curiosity.

"Could be," Mary said. "He's seventy, if he's a day."

"That's no great age," I said as I competently rolled out dough for the buns and tucked the edges under. "Not in these times. Patent medicines can do wonders."

"Lord Alfred loves his dad, that's for certain," Mary went on. "Is ever so gentle with him."

Jane, who'd listened to much of the conversation in sullen silence, let out a snort. "That ain't true. Lord Alfred wants to be marquess, not just a marquess's son."

"Lord Alfred is too kind for that," Mary said insistently. From the flush on her cheek, I deduced she had a fondness for Lord Alfred.

"You think the best of everybody, Mary," Jane sneered. "'Cause you're a fool."

"Now, Jane, mind your tongue," I admonished. I agreed with her that Mary was a bit too quick to trust, but Jane's philosophy seemed to be to dislike everyone on sight.

I wondered what had happened to give Jane such anger. The likes of us had to drudge for a living, and while some complained, others did it cheerfully and managed to live a happy life. I concluded that more than hard labor had turned Jane bitter.

"Lord Babcock must have had his children later in life,"

I mused. "If Lord Alfred and Lady Margaret are not yet thirty."

"His first wife had trouble carrying little ones," Mary said. "Lost a few before Lord Alfred and Lady Margaret came along, and it was touch and go with both of them. That's how the first Lady Babcock died, so it's said. Trying for another child."

"How very sad," I said in sudden sympathy. "That must have been difficult for the family."

"That's not what *everyone* says," Jane broke in with a scowl at Mary. "Some say Lord Babcock poisoned the first Lady Babcock so he could marry the second one. She was young then, quite a beauty in her day, I'm told."

"A lady who miscarried children and had trouble bearing them likely was weakened by it," I said. "It is not surprising that the first Lady Babcock died. Not every death is helped along by poison, even if it might seem unexpected. A person's constitution can be a complicated thing."

My mother had been a robust woman, but working so hard to keep us in bread and butter, not to mention the rent for our tiny rooms, had worn her down. When her illness came, she hadn't had any strength left to fight it.

I busily formed more rolls, willing my eyes to remain dry.

"What about your patent medicines that keep a body fit?" Jane asked with sarcasm.

I sent her an admonishing frown, both in disapproval and to disguise my emotions. "Do not be so impertinent, Jane. Have you finished with those carrots?"

Jane shoved a plate of them to me, cut into a perfect

dice. I admit, the reason I didn't send Jane off on errands that would get her out of the kitchen was that she was proving quite competent at her job.

Mary, on the other hand, fumbled even at stirring a batter, more interested in chattering. I kept her sorting and stacking dishes and pans when she wasn't washing them. Mostly, she rested her hip against the table and talked while we worked.

"Excellent," I told Jane. "Now please do the same with the parsnips. They'll make a fine addition to the ham."

Jane made a face at me but fell to chopping once more.

———

When I served the staff their supper that night, I observed a softening in belligerence toward me. The three footmen shoveled in the pork, potatoes, and soft buns slathered in butter with great enjoyment, and even Mrs. Seabrook gave me a grudging, *I suppose you do know something about cooking.*

I did not hear from Armitage, who snatched a plate and shut himself in his butler's pantry, but the dish that Mary brought back from him had been scraped clean.

Jane said nothing at all as we ate our meal in the kitchen, but she ceased glowering at me and helped herself to two buns.

After we finished, I took a basket of food scraps up to the street, as was my habit, to give to any lingering beggars.

To my surprise, the men and women who usually

waited for me outside the Mount Street house had turned up here. Word had spread of my whereabouts, I supposed.

After I'd emptied the basket, I walked a little way down the road to a figure who huddled beneath a tree near the railings to the square's park.

"I suppose you've come to look after me," I said to the motionless lump. "And told these others to as well."

Daniel unfolded to his full height, shrugging off the tattered blanket he'd pulled around his shoulders. "I will always look out for you, Kat."

I did not like the warmth that filled me at his words. I kept my tone brisk. "If you wish to be useful, will you find something out for me?" I pulled the cup I'd hidden from the bottom of the basket. "Will you have someone test the substance in here for me? I believe it is only laudanum, but I want to be certain."

CHAPTER 5

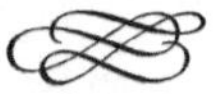

Daniel's nonchalance faded in an instant. "Why?" he asked, tone sharp.

"Someone dosed the cook. I want to know whether it was out of concern for her health or something more sinister."

Daniel took the cup and peered at the dregs inside, though he could scarcely see them in this light. "Why would someone want to poison the cook?"

"I don't know, do I?" I demanded. "That is why I wish to be certain. Her ladyship—or whoever prepared the tea —perhaps wished to aid her to rest. My fancy might be wrong."

"Your ideas usually aren't wrong." Daniel folded a handkerchief around the cup and tucked it into his pocket. "I will have this looked at right away and tell you the results tomorrow." He put a hand on my arm. "I don't like you in a house where people are dropping laudanum into teacups on a whim."

"Do not worry—I am careful." I decided I would not

upset him with the fact that I'd discovered the doctored tea by drinking it myself. "Who on earth will you have test the substance late on the Saturday night before Easter?"

Daniel shrugged. "I know a number of men for whom one day is the same as another. Thanos, for instance, will break into a chemical lab at the Polytechnic if I ask him to."

"He mustn't get into any trouble," I said quickly. "He was invited to Easter dinner with Lady Cynthia and the Bywaters, though I do not know if the invitation will extend to him coming to Lord Babcock's meal. Rather unfair." My annoyance at the situation resurged.

"I doubt he'll mind." Daniel flashed a smile. "His greatest disappointment would be not dining with Lady Cynthia, but he'll mend."

"It was highly inconvenient to all of us," I growled. "But never mind. What's done is done. I will prepare a fine dinner and then go home."

"After you discover why the cook was given laudanum, of course." Daniel's eyes twinkled in the faint gaslight from the road.

I frowned at him. "Do go away if you will only tease me."

Daniel laughed, which loosened me enough to smile back at him.

He ceased his laughter abruptly, stepped to me, and caught my mouth in a kiss.

I was too surprised to stop him, and truth to tell, I did not want to. I savored the warmth of it until Daniel eased back and regarded me with an unreadable look.

"Good night, Kat," he said softly.

"Good night, Daniel." I quickly turned and took my leave before I'd be tempted to stay.

———

I SLEPT that night in a tiny room next to the butler's pantry, which had obviously once been used for storing wine and other foodstuffs. The wine bottles were gone, but their racks remained, a bunk shoved into the narrow space between them. The nook was set up for when extra help was needed in the house, Mrs. Seabrook explained to me.

There was no room for Tess. Mary offered to let her bunk in with herself, Jane, and a downstairs maid, but Jane made her disapprobation known.

"I can barely sleep with you two kicking me," Jane told Mary. "I don't need a third pair of feet at me."

"Tess can return to Mount Street for the night and walk back in the morning," I intervened. "It is no great distance."

That was true, but the night had grown dark, and Tess glanced nervously at the high windows. I helped her into her coat and guided her to the back door.

"Daniel is lurking," I whispered to her. "He'll see you home safe."

Tess brightened at my words. "I'll be here first thing," she promised before she slipped out.

I hoped she'd treat herself to a good long rest, which was more than I'd obtain on the lumpy cot.

I was proved correct about the bed's discomfort. I woke very early in the morning, out of sorts, but washed my face and hands, donned my clothes and apron, and entered the kitchen ready to work.

No one was stirring yet, and I got much done before the others, including Tess, arrived an hour later. Mary and Jane were surprised that I had bread baking and hash frying for our breakfast, as well as the ham basted and ready for the oven. Tess, used to my morning efficiency, simply hung up her hat and tied on her apron.

"Daniel has news for you," Tess murmured to me when we had a moment alone.

"Is he outside?" I hoped so. A chat with Daniel would be a refreshing reprieve in an otherwise hectic morning.

Tess shook her head. "He says that nice Mr. Thanos is coming to dinner, and he'll tell you."

"Good." I was disappointed I wouldn't be able to rush up to the street and confer with Daniel, but I'd be glad to see Mr. Thanos. I was also happy he'd not be cheated out of his Easter dinner.

I had little time to ponder about what Mr. Thanos might have to say. After a quick repast, we cooked breakfast for those upstairs before continuing with the main meal of the day.

Breakfast for those above stairs meant plenty of fresh bread, toasted muffins with butter, a tureen of poached eggs, and some of the potato hash I'd made for the staff. A tray with a small amount of all of this went up via Mrs. Seabrook to the lady of the house for breakfast in bed, while the rest of the family would help themselves from the dishes at the sideboard.

Mrs. Seabrook paused to study the tray I'd prepared for Lady Babcock. "It looks edible," she said. She hadn't yet sampled any breakfast, declaring it was her duty to serve her ladyship first.

"It's delicious, Mrs. Seabrook," Mary assured her. "At least the hash and the bread. Mrs. Holloway is a fine cook."

Mrs. Seabrook glanced at Jane, who was less likely to gush at everything. "Best breakfast I've et in a good bit," she said grudgingly.

Mrs. Seabrook lifted her brows but said nothing more as she continued out with the tray.

I set Jane to slicing potatoes Mary had diligently scrubbed, while Tess and I washed and tore apart the greens, which we'd keep crisp in water until they were served. I slid the ham from the oven to add the carrots, onions, parsnips, and celery to the juices and set it all back in to continue roasting alongside the shank of mutton. The quail, which would take less time to roast, I dressed and added to the oven. As there were only six of them, these would have to be sliced apart to be shared as small servings.

The fish I'd ordered had been delivered, as fishermen, like domestics, were unable to take many holidays. In addition to the ham, mutton, and quail, we'd have the first courses of oxtail soup and poached sole, then croquettes with a soubise sauce, which was a white sauce seasoned with cayenne and onions, to which I added a bit of bacon for a smoky flavor.

For the desserts, I set Mary to whipping cream—something uncomplicated for her—which I then sweetened with a touch of sugar. I sliced the strawberries myself to set on the cake that had survived the journey from Mount Street.

The pastries also needed to be iced, the ham basted, and stocks made into gravies and sauces. We bustled from table to oven to dresser and back, while Mary, once she'd whipped the cream to perfection, carried loads of pots and dishes to her sink in the scullery.

Mrs. Seabrook returned. "Her ladyship devoured her breakfast," she declared. "First time in a long while."

I was pleased she liked it. "How is Mrs. Morgan?" I'd sent a bit of hash and toasted muffin upstairs via Mary earlier, and she'd said the cook was awake though still weak.

"Too much to do this morning to look in on her," Mrs. Seabrook snapped and marched out, though she slid the plate of food I'd prepared for her from the table as she went. We soon heard the slam of the door to the house-keeper's parlor.

I was far too busy to look in on Mrs. Morgan myself, but I told Mary to nip upstairs and retrieve the tray. I'd put a hearty cup of tea, one without laudanum, on it, with instructions to Mary that the cook was not to drink or eat anything that I didn't send her myself.

Mary returned while Tess was removing another fresh-baked loaf from the oven, the bread's odor inviting.

"Cook et it all." Mary showed me the tray with its empty plates. "She's feeling a bit better, but I don't think she'll be down to help us today."

That was just as well, I decided. Two strong-minded cooks in one kitchen simply got in each other's way.

"She says she wants to have a chat with you soon," Mary went on. "She's worried about the dinner, I think."

We were well into the most critical parts of the meal, everything needing to come together in a moment, so I could not rush upstairs and reassure Mrs. Morgan right now. I'd wait until the last course went upstairs, then I'd take her a piece of strawberry cake and tell her that all was well.

I was pleased that we'd begun moving like a well-oiled machine, differences put aside in the rush to finish the meal. Even Jane ceased her antagonism and quietly chopped, stirred, and iced what I put in front of her. Tess was invaluable with her knowledge of what needed to be tended first, which she'd learned in her years of working for me.

Mary, who left her sink from time to time to scurry halfway up the outside stairs, reported on the guests' arrivals.

"There's that pretty Lady Cynthia, with her aunt and uncle," Mary announced when she descended. "I hear she wears trousers, but she's in a frock like anyone else." She sounded disappointed. "A black-haired man came with them. Maybe her sweetheart?"

Mr. Thanos, I thought in relief. Mrs. Bywater hadn't, in the end, stopped him coming. Mr. Thanos got along well with almost everyone, so I didn't worry about him much.

Other guests included a bishop in a purple waistcoat and dog collar, one of the Babcocks' cousins, a few ladies and gentlemen who were friends of Lord Alfred and Lady Margaret, and Lady Babcock's maiden aunt. *A commoner,* Mrs. Seabrook sniffed on her way through. *Nobody.*

Mr. and Mrs. Bywater were commoners as well, I reflected, but they were blood related to a daughter of an earl, so perhaps they were spared Mrs. Seabrook's complete disdain. I'd already heard Mrs. Seabrook refer to Mrs. Bywater as *Lady Babcock's silly friend,* which meant she didn't think much of her, in any case.

Mrs. Seabrook said that the guests would converse in the drawing room with whatever drinks Lord Babcock served them, then they'd move to the dining room.

In the kitchen, we hurriedly put the soup into the dumbwaiter, and I cranked it upstairs to where Armitage, who'd slid into a frock coat and hurried up a quarter of an hour ago, would be poised to retrieve it.

The fish went up soon after, and then the ham came out of the oven in all its glory.

I refused to let the others help me transfer it to the large platter that would be its final resting place. I settled the platter on a tray then added roasted potatoes, spring cherries in aspic, and a pot of the jelly sauce that would accompany it all.

I carried the tray carefully to the dumbwaiter, while Tess, Mary, and Jane watched proudly. I had just slid the ham and its trimmings into the dumbwaiter's box and shut its door when Mrs. Seabrook hastened into the kitchen.

"Put it all away," Mrs. Seabrook commanded. "The dinner is off."

I froze with my fingers around the dumbwaiter's door handle, certain I hadn't heard her aright. Tess and Jane fell equally silent behind me. The outburst, when it came, was from Mary.

"What d'ya mean it's off?" she screeched. "We worked ever so hard. I scrubbed all them tatties!"

I heard Mrs. Seabrook's swift movement and swung around in time to seize her upraised arm before she could strike Mary, who flinched away from her.

"What has happened?" I demanded, releasing the indignant Mrs. Seabrook. At least she let her hand fall and did not try again to hit Mary. "A family does not dismiss an entire meal on a whim, especially not on a feast day. Is someone ill?"

Mrs. Seabrook drew herself up. "Lord Alfred has died," she told me in a hard voice.

The four of us stared at her in shock. Mrs. Seabrook's eyes were red-rimmed, and her breath came fast.

Died? I repeated to myself. Lord Alfred, the marquess's heir, was a young man, as Mary had informed us.

Mary gasped in stunned dismay. "His young lordship? Can't be. You've made a mistake."

Mrs. Seabrook rounded on her as though she'd box Mary's ears, but fortunately, she did no such thing. "It is not a mistake, you stupid girl. He is dead, and his lordship has canceled the meal."

"Poor man." Tess was the only one of us jarred out of our amazement to express sympathy. "Was he sickly? Or frail? Sometimes people just fall over, like, no matter how young."

"He weren't frail." Mary scoffed. "His young lordship is robust and hearty. Rides every morning, don't he? So handsome, always with a kind word for me. It must have been the fish." Her voice broke, and she buried her face in her apron and began to weep.

"It was *not* the fish," I said immediately. Cooks were prone to be the first blamed when someone grew peaky over their supper. "It was delivered fresh, and I checked it thoroughly. It was sweet as can be. I taste every dish before it's plated, and I am right as rain."

"He never ate the fish, you silly woman," Mrs. Seabrook snapped. "He was wandering about the hall as they all went into dine, telling me his stomach was a bit achy and that the others should begin without him. I was clearing up in the drawing room when I heard the front door open, but no one was announced. When I came out to see who the footman had admitted, I found the door wide open and Lord Alfred dead on the floor."

Mrs. Seabrook drew a sharp breath, as though the impact of finding him was just coming to her. She needed a strong cup of tea, though I was too dazed to pour her one at the moment.

Mary continued to sob, but Jane was utterly still, her face draining of color until it was nearly green.

"Did his heart give out?" Tess asked gently. "I had a cousin who swore he was only dyspeptic one day, but he died that evening, sleeping in a chair by the fire."

"I doubt it," Mrs. Seabrook retorted. "He was stabbed, wasn't he? A tramp, who'd been skulking about outside all night, came right into our house and struck him with a knife. Now, take away all this food, Mrs. Holloway. We won't be needing it."

CHAPTER 6

*A*s soon as Mrs. Seabrook marched out of the kitchen, the three kitchen maids began to babble simultaneously.

"Is it really true?" Mary scrubbed her face with her apron. "Should we run for a constable?"

"A constable, yes, if he were murdered," Tess said. "I can go." I knew she meant to seek Caleb, who would be on his beat around Mount Street today.

"It were never a tramp that killed him." This last came from Jane, who still appeared rather sickly.

"Why do you say that, Jane?" I asked.

Jane shrugged, her sullenness returning. "Why should a tramp march inside and stick a knife into the first person he sees?"

"Because he's a madman," Mary wailed. "Poor Lord Alfred. We ain't safe here, not if they could do that to the poor young master." Her sobs continued.

"Mary." I made my voice cut through her hysteria. "Take

the rest of the rolls from the oven before they burn. Use the towels so you don't scorch your hands and set the pan on top of the stove. Jane, carry the ham back to the table. We'll divide up the vegetables among us staff, because they won't last, and we'll send up the aspic and slices of ham to put on the sideboard in the dining room. The family will be hungry, even through this tragedy. Tess, please go out and find Mr. McAdam and tell him what's happened."

I assumed the tramp Mrs. Seabrook claimed had been lurking all night was Daniel. Why he had nothing better to do than linger in Portman Square, I did not know, but I was grateful he'd remained.

"Who's Mr. McAdam?" Jane asked in sudden suspicion.

"Someone who might be able to help. Take care with that tray, Jane. It is heavy."

"I know that." Jane's lip curled as she carried the ham to the table, but she was cautious while crossing the floor. She set down the ham amid the pile of cakes and pastries we'd readied. "What's going to become of it all? Mary ain't wrong. We worked our fingers to the bone."

I watched Tess remove her apron and scuttle out, wishing I could go with her. "It sometimes happens, unfortunately," I said to Jane. "We will store what we can for the family to eat, though I'm certain my mistress will insist that anything we brought returns with us."

"Sounds like your mistress is a right cow," Jane declared.

A light female voice answered her. "That is possibly true."

Jane swung around, her face going scarlet as Lady Cynthia walked briskly into the kitchen.

Cynthia surveyed our mess and shook her head in sympathy. "My, my, what a waste. You are quite right, Mrs. H. Auntie sent me down here to tell you we must pack up all the food and wine and take it home to Mount Street. Not one morsel to be missed, she said."

Jane dropped a contrite curtsey. "Sorry, my lady."

"Quite all right," Lady Cynthia said. "That is Auntie all over, isn't it? Also, I'm dying of hunger. The soup was tasty, but I barely had a bite before Lady Babcock lays down her spoon and tells the footmen to serve the fish. Had maybe two bites of that before Mrs. Seabrook raised the alarm about poor Alfred. I thought Lady Babcock would faint dead away, but the rest of the family and guests ignored her in their stampede to the hall. Lord Babcock is beside himself with grief, as you can imagine, but he's resisting sending for the police, saying it will do no good."

"Please sit down, my lady." I gestured Cynthia to the least cluttered corner of the table and drew the best chair to it. I took up my knife and sliced a few pieces of ham for her and fetched one of the buns Mary had just removed from the oven. "Tuck into that," I told her as I set the plate in front of her and spooned sauce over all. "Tess has gone to tell Daniel."

"Good for her." Cynthia snatched up a fork with enthusiasm. "You don't mind if Thanos comes down as well, do you? He's hovering at the top of the stairs, uncertain of his welcome in the kitchen but not wanting to intrude on the family either. I had the excuse of Auntie to enter your sanctuary."

This kitchen was hardly a sanctuary, but I knew what Cynthia meant. I sliced off a few more pieces of ham. "Of course he is welcome."

"Excellent. I'll fetch him."

"No need," I said quickly as she started to rise. "I will invite him down. You enjoy your meal."

Cynthia settled in again and lifted her fork. "Don't mind if I do. I feel terrible wanting to eat when someone has just killed poor Alfred, but for some reason I'm famished. Excellent ham, Mrs. H."

Jane watched Lady Cynthia in some trepidation, Mary peeking in from the scullery to which she'd retreated.

I thanked Cynthia for her compliment then hastened to the backstairs and up them. I wanted to tow Mr. Thanos to the kitchen before Mrs. Seabrook or Armitage saw him and chivvied him somewhere, possibly out of the house.

When I opened the green baize door, I found Mr. Thanos near it. He stood still, peering toward the front of the house and the wide hall where I assumed Lord Alfred had met his demise.

The floor was polished walnut, dark with a fine sheen, no rug to mar its surface. The front door led into a foyer, which had another door between it and the main hall. The foyer's door, with stained glass in its upper half, stood open, though the front door was now closed.

The hall flowed past one large set of closed double doors, which I assumed led to the drawing room. The staircase came next, rising gracefully to the next floor.

Opposite the staircase was another set of doors. One of these was open, giving me a glimpse of the dining room, which was still filled with people in fine clothes. The gentlemen wore black suits and sharp white cravats, while the ladies were in gowns of light spring colors.

The inhabitants were extraordinarily silent, though I saw one gentleman pouring brandy at the sideboard. I presumed none of them knew exactly what to do.

Of Albert's body, there was no sign. Nor did I see any blood staining the perfection of the floor.

Mr. Thanos too wore a black suit, though his cravat was crooked and one of his waistcoat buttons had come undone. I was used to seeing him in plainer suits of flannel or wool, but black broadcloth suited his slim figure, dark hair, and soft brown eyes.

"Mr. Thanos?"

At the sound of my voice, Mr. Thanos jumped, his feet nearly coming off the floor before he spun to face me.

"Oh, Mrs. Holloway." He pressed a hand to his heart. "You startled me."

I gestured to the front hall. "Is that where …?" I whispered the question, not wanting Mrs. Bywater, who I caught sight of in the dining room, to realize I was upstairs.

Mr. Thanos nodded. "Gave me quite a jolt to rush out here and see the poor chap crumpled to the floor. He'd greeted me in the drawing room not a half hour ago, and he was breezy and trying to be witty, though he said his stomach was troubling him. Stabbed, the housekeeper said. Front door was wide open. They've moved him into the drawing room." He waved a hand at the closed doors.

"No one was stationed in the foyer?" Usually, in fine houses, a footman was assigned to stand at the front door so they could help guests from carriages and usher them inside. They also safeguarded the house from any would-be intruders.

"No, no, Lady Babcock had all the footmen in the dining room serving. Too many guests for her number of staff, Cyn mused to me in a whisper."

"The front door was left unlocked while no one was there to stand guard?" I asked in wonderment.

"I suppose." Mr. Thanos blinked. "I really have no idea."

"I see no blood," I remarked. Not that I wanted to gaze upon such a thing, but it was strange.

"Yes, I noticed that. He was lying on a rug, which the three footmen lifted and carried into the drawing room with Lord Alfred on it. He's still in there, stretched across the sofa."

Which meant Alfred hadn't bled enough for it to seep through the rug to the boards beneath.

Mr. Thanos drew a breath. "Such a shock. Truth to tell, I am glad you have popped out, Mrs. Holloway. I meant to tell you, I discovered what was in the teacup. There were barely enough dregs to make a study, but one of my chums at the Polytechnic is a clever chap. He could isolate the various components of air itself if he could put it into a beaker. And I believe he can. You have to—"

"What was in the tea, Mr. Thanos?" Sometimes rudely interrupting Mr. Thanos was the only way to gain information.

"Eh? Oh, yes. I beg your pardon. It wasn't laudanum. It was morphine."

He gazed at me in triumph, but I was no more enlightened.

"Morphine?" I repeated dubiously. "I've heard of it. It's a sort of medicine, isn't it?"

"Yes, it can alleviate pain, but too much is quite deadly. Mixing it with alcohol or something like laudanum will speed up its effects, but one can die in a few minutes from having even a small dose."

Cold flashed through me. "A mercy I only had a swallow, then."

His eyes widened. "You drank some? Good heavens, yes, it is a mercy. Also, the tea diluted it a good bit, according to my friend. I am happy to see you alive and well, Mrs. Holloway."

My knees were shaky, and I put my hand on the wall to steady myself. "Thank you for finding out, Mr. Thanos."

"Not at all. Are you well?" He regarded me with concern in his kindly dark eyes.

"Yes, I will be." I hadn't drunk more of the tea, and I was quite fine, after all. No need to break down.

The question remained, who had dosed the tea for Mrs. Morgan and why? Had her initial illness been true, or also caused by a dollop of morphine?

I drew a breath, remembering my errand. "Come downstairs with me. Lady Cynthia is there, and I know you haven't had enough to eat."

Mr. Thanos gave me another concerned glance but followed me to the backstairs door, reaching to open it for me before I could. He could not help always being the gentleman, even to a cook.

By the time we reached the kitchen, Tess had returned. "I told him," she whispered to me as I began to fix Mr. Thanos a plate. "He sent me back here and hurried off."

I nodded at her in thanks and carried Mr. Thanos's meal to him.

He rubbed his hands. "Seems callous to want food at a time like this, but thank you, Mrs. Holloway."

"I said the same thing," Cynthia stated. She and Mr. Thanos shared a tiny smile of camaraderie, which pleased me beneath my bewilderment.

I agreed with Jane that a tramp swarming into a fine home on Portman Square and stabbing the young master to death as he happened to cross the hall was an unlikely occurrence. Constables walked their beats in these parts, even on Easter Sunday, and one would be certain to notice a vagrant looking for unlocked doors.

The idea came to me that perhaps the open door was a blind, and someone already in the house had decided to do away with the young master. One of the guests enraged with him? A servant, such as Armitage, who might strike out in a drunken stupor if Lord Alfred argued with him?

I would more believe it the work of an intruder, if it weren't for Mrs. Morgan. She'd been afraid for some reason, and the tea intended for her had been laced with poison. Had Lady Babcock wanted Mrs. Morgan sunk into a long stupor or perhaps out of the way entirely?

Mrs. Seabrook had mentioned that Mrs. Morgan and Lady Babcock had been quarreling "something fierce," speculating it was over the menus. But Lord Alfred's death cast a more sinister shadow on the arguments. Had Mrs. Morgan realized that Lady Babcock meant to do away with her stepson? Tried to persuade her against it? Therefore, Mrs. Morgan had to be taken out of the way?

Then again, I reasoned, Lady Babcock might not have tampered with Mrs. Morgan's tea at all. If she'd set the cup down somewhere between wherever she'd brewed it and the cook's bedchamber, anyone could have slipped the poison into it.

Anyone in the house at the time, I amended. Which meant the servants and the rest of the family.

I had no idea how difficult it was to get hold of morphine. Was it something only a doctor could dispense, or did one walk into the nearest chemist's shop and request it? Mrs. Seabrook had mentioned that a doctor did give Lady Babcock medicine, but she hadn't specified what.

These were questions the police would have to ask, as it was not my place, but the two events narrowed down the list of suspects.

Then again, the incidents might be entirely unconnected. Lady Babcock, in her rather dim way, might have been trying to nurse Mrs. Morgan back to health, and had nothing to do with whoever had killed Lord Alfred.

Watch out for her, Mrs. Morgan had urged me.

Because she thought the woman might kill her stepson?

I needed to know who had been in or outside of the dining room when Lord Alfred had died.

Under the pretense of packing up the food, I moved to

the table near Cynthia and Mr. Thanos so I could have a low-voiced conversation with them.

"Who were the guests today?" I asked Cynthia.

Her light blue eyes went wide. "Good Lord, are you thinking one of them killed Alfie while we were enjoying our soup?"

"It is one possibility," I said cautiously.

"Well, let me see." Cynthia's eyes narrowed in thought. "There's Margaret, of course, Alfie's sister. Another member of the family turned up—Desmond Charlton. Third cousin, I believe. Margaret is batty about him. Wants to marry the fellow, though Lady Babcock doesn't approve of the match. Desmond and his brother haven't much money, at least, not enough for Desmond to marry Margaret and keep her in the manner to which she is accustomed. Then there was a bishop, whose name I can't remember—"

"Norris," Mr. Thanos supplied.

"Norris," Cynthia repeated. "A few friends Margaret invited that I know fairly well myself—Catherine and Thomas Bowler, who have recently made a match. Alice Hodgkinson and her sister Caroline, who are of eligible age, probably brought to entice Alfred to propose to one of them. Their brother Cuthbert, who was likely there as a potential husband for Margaret. As I say, Lady Babcock doesn't like Margaret's attachment to Third Cousin Desmond, so she's always matchmaking for Margaret. Auntie and Uncle, of course. Thanos. Me. Oh, and Lady Babcock's aunt, whose name I also can't remember."

"Miss Jordan," Mr. Thanos said.

"That's it. Jordan. She faded into the woodwork, as

though she didn't want anyone to notice her. Not that I blame her. Both Margaret and Alfred were rather rude to her."

Mrs. Seabrook had referred to Miss Jordan scoffingly as a nobody. I imagined the son and daughter of the house thought the same, especially as they didn't seem pleased with their stepmother.

Her ladyship ain't wanted, Mrs. Morgan had said about Lady Babcock. *No one can stick her.*

I wondered why Lady Babcock had invited her aunt when she herself wasn't welcome in her own husband's house. But perhaps Miss Jordan hadn't had anywhere else to go for Easter. Perhaps the woman thought it better to suffer some rudeness in exchange for an excellent dinner than to sit alone at home.

I myself would rather fix a simple meal and enjoy my own company, but others did not have such fortitude. And perhaps Miss Jordan didn't have the means for even a simple meal. The upper classes were full of impoverished and forgotten gentlewomen.

"All remained in the dining room?" I asked as I laid Mr. Davis's unopened wine bottles into their crates. "For the first part of the meal?"

"Once we were being served, yes," Cynthia answered. "Before that, we rather drifted about. Foul-tasting ratafia in the drawing room, though I longed for a stiff whiskey. Then we wandered from there to the dining room, no gentlemen taking in the ladies or anything like that. Very informal, and rather haphazard, which is how Lady Babcock prefers things. My aunt had much to say about that, but I like Lady Babcock. An uncomplicated woman."

"Any of us could have lingered to stab Lord Alfred, I suppose," Mr. Thanos said. "I can't say who exactly was in the dining room at any one time except myself and Cynthia, of course, before the soup was served." He blenched. "What a horrible thought. No, it *must* have been an intruder, don't you think?"

Mr. Thanos's words and expression pleaded with me to agree. Much easier to believe an anonymous person of the streets had broken into the house and done murder, than someone one had sat down to a meal with.

"I find it odd that the front door was left unlocked and unbolted when there was no footman to guard it," I said.

"Exactly," Cynthia agreed. "Very likely it wasn't unlocked at all, and the murderer opened it to make it seem so. Which means, Thanos, it must have been one of the dining party, I'm sorry to say. The bishop is a shifty cove, I've always thought."

I could not tell whether she'd have believed such a thing if Alfred hadn't been murdered. But then, not all members of the clergy were upright beings. Some were given livings based solely on their connections rather than any religious leanings.

"I also find it odd that Lord Babcock wants it kept quiet," I said. "Lord Alfred is his son and heir. Shouldn't he want to know who murdered him?"

"Yes, but what a scandal if it's known Alfie was killed in his own house," Cynthia answered. "They'll never live it down. I'll wager Lord Babcock will put about that Alfie died of sudden illness and swear us to secrecy."

"Or, his lordship already knows who killed him." I firmly set a lid onto the box of wine. "And wants to spare that person the gallows." Would he stand by his own wife, I wondered. If she'd murdered his beloved son?

"You don't suppose Lord Babcock killed Alfie himself?" Cynthia's brows rose. "That can't be, can it? What man would kill his own son?"

"'Cause maybe he ain't his son." Jane had paused in her duties to listen, and now she dropped this interesting bit into the conversation.

"Why on earth would you say that?" I demanded. I ought to admonish Jane for eavesdropping, interrupting, and stating such slander, but I was too curious to be very outraged.

"The first Lady Babcock had many beaus, so they say," Jane said without compunction. "Wasn't pure as the driven snow when she married his lordship. I've heard it was put about that his young lordship wasn't actually the marquess's son."

"That's not true," Mary flashed, also having drifted to us. "He's a fine young man—" She broke off, tears filling her eyes, as though she realized she now had to speak of Lord Alfred in the past tense.

"Oh, he's the son of an aristo, all right, but which one?" Jane said darkly. "Begging your pardon, your ladyship."

"Never mind … Jane, is it?" Cynthia said. "I've heard that rumor myself, but I think it's all rot. Alfie resembles —resembled—Lord Babcock quite a bit, so no one officially questioned Alfie's legitimacy. The first Lady Babcock took that secret to her grave, if it was even true, so we shall never know."

"It is of no matter anymore," I pointed out gently.

"Who will inherit Lord Babcock's title now? Third Cousin Desmond?"

Cynthia shook her head as she chewed a mouthful of ham and aspic. "Desmond's older brother, Stephan. He's not here today, as he is in France for reasons that are not clear. Desmond is representing their branch of the family. With Alfie out of the way, Stephan is the heir, Desmond the spare." She coughed and reached for the glass of wine I'd poured for her. "I say, you don't mean that *Stephan* did it? Disguised himself as a tramp and all that and stabbed Alfie? To clear the way for their twig of the family tree?"

"Anything is possible," I said with a shrug.

As I'd learned through helping Daniel investigate crimes, the police were usually less concerned with *why* a person was killed than proving who had done it. There was plenty of motivation for murder—a person might be a wealthy man who would bequeath a large sum when dead, or he'd aggravated the wrong person too many times, or he was the victim of a robbery or some other random crime.

In Lord Alfred's case, he stood in the way of another man inheriting a title and an estate. Illegitimate children could not inherit, of course, no matter what, but if no one *knew* Lord Alfred was illegitimate, or no one could prove it—or if it wasn't true at all—then there wasn't much any doubters could do. But perhaps there was enough shame or fear of the truth that someone in the family had decided to make the question irrelevant. Now this Stephan would inherit, and his brother had been conveniently in the house.

Or perhaps Lord Alfred had simply angered someone,

who'd struck out in rage, whether they'd meant to kill him or not.

How they'd managed to kill the man while everyone had been in sight of each other in the dining room was another problem.

Not that I would have the chance to look into the matter. This was not my kitchen or my house. I was being bundled back to Mount Street as unceremoniously as I'd been bundled to Portman Square.

Armitage put an end to our conversation by storming rather unsteadily into the kitchen.

"Are you still here?" he demanded of me. "You'd better clear out right quick, Mrs. Cook. The police have arrived, and they're questioning everyone in the house, like the bastards they are."

CHAPTER 7

*H*aving delivered his message, Armitage stamped down the passageway to his butler's pantry and slammed the door.

Jane's face went tight. "The police? I can't have no dealings with the police."

Why not? I wondered. Guilty conscience? And about what?

"I will not let them question you without me by your side," I promised her.

I'd learned from experience that constables or sergeants weren't always kind to servants, often assuming one of them was the culprit from the outset. Any reported theft or murder in a home led police directly to the staff. With the entire dinner party in the dining room digging into the fish, that left any servant wandering the house as a suspect.

Which included Mrs. Seabrook, I reminded myself. She'd claimed to be tidying up the drawing room and heard the front door open. She could have quietly stabbed Lord Alfred, opening the door to hint at an intruder.

Despite Lord Babcock's wishes, the police were here now. Tess had reported to Daniel, who'd have gone straight to Scotland Yard. We'd watched from the stairs outside the scullery while men in severe suits carried out Lord Alfred's body on a draped stretcher and loaded it into a van, presumably to take to a morgue. Mary had renewed her weeping as they went.

Lord Babcock had walked out with his son. He was a tall man, but his frame was bowed with grief. He rested a hand on the stretcher before the bearers loaded it, as though saying good-bye.

My eyes filled with tears as I watched. Poor man.

I had hoped that Inspector McGregor would be called upon to run the investigation. Though he disliked my interference, he'd believe me if I told him the kitchen staff had been with me working hard while the crime had been committed.

I heard McGregor's rumbling tones outside as we returned to the kitchen, but it wasn't he who descended below stairs to interview the staff. It was Sergeant Scott.

I'd first met Detective Sergeant Scott when he'd detained Lady Cynthia's father last fall in connection with a murder. The sergeant was a tall, youngish man with a sharp face, fair hair slicked against his skull, and shrewd blue eyes that took in everything around him.

If the sergeant was surprised to encounter me in this house, he made absolutely no sign of it. He instructed me to send in the kitchen servants to speak to him one at a time in the housekeeper's parlor before walking purposefully there and closing the door.

Cynthia and Mr. Thanos had retreated upstairs after Armitage's announcement, as they would be interviewed as well. They'd sent me sympathetic glances as they went but could no longer help me.

I decided to approach Sergeant Scott first. I entered the housekeeper's parlor to find a small room containing a few comfortable chairs, a writing desk, and a sideboard with a half-full carafe of wine reposing on it.

Sergeant Scott had pulled the desk away from the wall so he could face his suspects and had set a chair in front of it for those he'd interrogate. He did not look up when I entered, only continued scribbling into a small notebook.

I declined the silently offered chair, preferring to stay on my feet. "Is Inspector McGregor speaking to the upstairs?" I asked before Sergeant Scott could address me. "He should be told that the footmen were instructed to be in the dining room, leaving the front door unguarded, which is a strange thing to do. Inspector McGregor might be wise to find out who gave the order."

Sergeant Scott continued writing for a moment, though whether he took note of my observation or ignored it, I couldn't say.

He at last fixed me with his pale blue gaze. "Mrs. Holloway, you are cook for a family in Mount Street, not this house."

No question of whether I'd changed my place of employment since I'd seen him last. He knew I didn't work here and waited for me to explain my presence.

"Lady Babcock's cook has taken ill. Mrs. Bywater volunteered my services."

His brows rose slightly. "Do you often cook for other households on your mistress's whim?"

"No," I said, a bit too quickly. "This was an unusual circumstance."

Sergeant Scott's pencil scratched on his page. "The nature of the cook's illness?"

"I don't really know. She is poorly, I can tell you that. The morphine given her can't help, can it?"

The pencil abruptly ceased. Sergeant Scott looked up at me again, his eyes even sharper. "What morphine?"

"It was introduced into her tea. I have no idea who put it there."

"How do you know she was given morphine? And that it was in the tea?" His skewering gaze told me the most likely answer was that I'd put it there myself.

"Because I accidentally drank it," I admitted. "Fortunately, only a small mouthful, but the effect was strong, and the tea was terribly bitter. I gave the cup to Mr. McAdam to test. The report I received was that there were trace amounts of morphine. I am not certain if the dose was meant to murder the cook, make her ill, or make her well. The lady of the house carried it to her, but that does not mean she put the morphine in it."

"You knew poison had been put into a cup of tea, and you didn't summon a constable?" Scott demanded.

In my younger days, I might have wilted before his accusing stare, but I'd grown strong. "I did inform the police, in a way. I gave the cup to Mr. McAdam. As I say, the morphine might have been put there for benevolent reasons. If Mr. McAdam had been alarmed, he'd have told Inspector McGregor."

"McAdam doesn't answer to McGregor," Sergeant Scott growled.

"I know," I replied as calmly as I could.

Daniel worked for a horrible man called Monaghan, but I had no idea how much Sergeant Scott discerned of the exact nature of Daniel's assignments. I knew very little myself, because Daniel wasn't allowed to tell me. Scott knew *something* of it, but it wasn't for me to babble about Daniel and the tasks Monaghan set him onto.

Sergeant Scott regarded me severely for a few more seconds, then returned to his book. "Describe the events of today, leading to the death of Lord Alfred Charlton."

"We were busy preparing the Easter dinner," I said. "Which is quite a long process. None of us left the kitchen, that I saw, once all the guests had arrived. Hours pass quickly when one is cooking, and it is a miracle we finish it all by the time the butler summons the diners. We had ham and its accompaniments, a mutton shank and some quail, all the vegetables, the fish and the soup, bread to go with every course, not to mention the pastries and tarts I'd been working on over the past week—"

"Given that you were paying close attention to your tasks," the sergeant interrupted me. "Could it be that you didn't notice anyone from downstairs nipping up to the main floors? Lord Alfred was fatally stabbed in the base of his neck. Death would have been very quick, and the murderer back in place before she was missed. You likely have a number of deadly knives in the kitchen. My constable is even now collecting them."

I briefly reflected that it was a mercy I'd decided against bringing my own. "Why did you say *she*?" I asked. "You suppose the murderer was a woman?"

"All the male servants were in the dining room, according to the butler," Sergeant Scott answered without hesitation. "That leaves the female servants unaccounted for."

"You wouldn't be so certain of the killer's gender if an intruder walked in and did it," I pointed out. "You are assuming someone in the house killed Lord Alfred?"

"I assume nothing, Mrs. Holloway. I only note what happened so the inspector will have as much information as possible to make an arrest."

His words were logical, but I was not reassured. "Lord Alfred was wandering the house, I've been told. He might have met his death *before* everyone was settled in the dining room, if one of the guests lingered to speak to him. You say it would have been very quick—how do you know he wasn't dead before the meal was served?"

Sergeant Scott's next glance told me he found me irritating and arrogant. "I will speak to the rest of the kitchen maids," he said, ignoring my question. "Their names?"

I bristled at his preemptory tone but answered without argument. "Tess Parsons, who is my assistant. Jane, the undercook, and Mary, scullery maid. I don't know their surnames, but Mrs. Seabrook will." As Sergeant Scott wrote this down, I continued, "I will remain while you question them. They're fearful, which is understandable."

"No, I will speak to them alone, without them looking to you for instruction on how to answer."

"I'll not abandon them, Sergeant," I said tightly.

Sergeant Scott frowned at me but remained cool. "You will not be—"

He broke off on a sudden, staring sharply at the door. I heard what he did, the sound of bottles clinking.

Scott rose and swiftly stepped past me. He wrenched open the door to reveal Armitage staggering into the hall with a large crate of wine bottles.

"You there," the sergeant demanded. "What are you doing?"

Armitage started, nearly dropping the box, but an answer sprang readily from his lips. "Moving the master's wine to a safe place. If there's a tramp lurking about, I need to make sure he don't nick anything, don't I?"

He lied—a few of those bottles were ones I'd brought that I hadn't finished packing. Armitage's safe place was likely one in which he'd either drink all the wine or sell it on.

Sergeant Scott detected the lie as well. "Put them down," he ordered.

"*I* didn't kill the young master. You're no one to tell me what to do—"

"*Now.*"

Armitage started again but after assessing the sergeant's impatience, he lowered the box to the slate floor. He straightened, one hand going to his back.

"*You* can answer to the master if they go missing," Armitage muttered both to me and the sergeant. "And put them all back. I have me duties to attend."

"I will speak to you soon," Sergeant Scott informed him. "Wait in there." He pointed to the butler's pantry.

Armitage began to splutter, but again, he wilted under Scott's cold stare. Armitage sent me a baleful glance but scuttled into the butler's pantry and slammed its door.

I moved around Sergeant Scott to peer into the box. "Half of those belong to the Mount Street house," I said. "May I take them?"

Sergeant Scott studied me without expression. I knew he did not give two sticks about who the wine belonged to, but he also knew that aristocrats were possessive of their expensive wine collections. He gave me a minute nod.

"Send in Miss Parsons when you go."

Without giving me a chance to answer, he stepped back into the housekeeper's parlor and closed the door with a decided click.

I'd never heft six bottles of wine under my arms, so I began to shove the crate down the hall toward the kitchen. I half expected Armitage to pop out and accuse me of theft, but he stayed put. Sergeant Scott, without ever raising his voice, had thoroughly intimidated him.

I was not as worried about Tess facing Sergeant Scott alone, despite some petty thieving in her past, because she'd grown less fearful about the police in the last few years. Her beau, Caleb Greene, was a constable, and she'd helped Daniel and me in some of our investigations. Tess had finally concluded that the Peelers were simply men doing a job, though there still were plenty of constables who thought nothing of bullying innocents.

I entered the kitchen half bent over the box I was pushing.

"You are next, Tess," I said breathlessly, and then added

for the benefit of the others, "Sergeant Scott can be aloof, but there's nothing to be frightened of. Just tell the truth. We were all here in the kitchen when the young master died."

I heard no response, so I straightened up, pushing tendrils of hair from my face. Tess and Mary regarded me with worry.

"I'm not afraid," Tess said. "But Jane's gone."

"Gone?" I shoved at another recalcitrant tendril. "What do you mean *gone?*"

"She legged it," Mary supplied. "Not ten seconds after you went into the room with Old Bill. She tore away her apron, and off she went."

CHAPTER 8

I uttered a few choice words under my breath as the other two watched me in trepidation.

Jane fleeing might have nothing to do with Lord Alfred's death, I told myself. The theory went that a guiltless person had no reason to run from the police, but I knew that in reality, plenty of people who'd done no wrong had been banged up, myself included. The instinct to take to one's heels was understandable.

Even so, it would be far better for Jane to stay and face Sergeant Scott than give him an excuse to arrest her.

"Tess, take our wine out of this crate and put it with what we brought," I said. "Then go down the hall and speak to Sergeant Scott. Mary, carry on with what you were doing, and under no circumstances allow Mr. Armitage to come in here and abscond with more bottles. I will find Jane."

So speaking, I removed my apron, snatched up my hat, and charged out of the house, taking the outside steps as rapidly as I could.

It was a bright, sunny Easter afternoon, perfect for families who lived on the square to stroll in Portman Square's small park, as many now did. Children smiled at mothers and fathers, who put aside their aristocratic arrogance to teach games to their sons and daughters, nannies hovering to ensure their charges were on their best behavior.

No one bothered to take note of a woman in cook's garb rushing along the street, searching every which way for an errant kitchen maid.

If Jane knew London well, she could be far away by now, gone to ground as only born-and-bred Londoners could. We might never see her again.

I doubted very much that Jane had stabbed Lord Alfred, but Sergeant Scott or Inspector McGregor might decide to arrest her in absentia and send out constables to scour the streets for her.

I headed down Orchard Street, reasoning that Jane would flee east and south as quickly as possible. She might have family or friends in that part of the metropolis or across the river who would take her in.

Long before I reached Oxford Street, I found Jane.

Or rather, I saw her struggling hard against Daniel, who was still dressed in his shabby clothes and trying to hold on to her.

I neared them just as Jane gave Daniel a hearty kick in the shin. Daniel winced, but his grip did not loosen.

"Stop," I commanded Jane.

She swung to me, her eyes wild. "Mrs. Holloway, help me get away from 'im. 'E's a madman."

"No, he is not. He is a friend, and you need to cease."

Jane's surprise stilled her. "A friend?" She studied Daniel in distaste. "What sort of friends you got, Missus?"

"Very good ones," I said. "Why are you trying to run, Jane? The sergeant will immediately suspect you're guilty, when I know you are not."

"Course I ain't. Who says I am? I never stuck a knife in the young master. Why should I? I keep myself well away from the likes of *'im*."

"Exactly," I said. "You were in view of me the whole time today, which I have already told Sergeant Scott. But taking flight will not help. Why did you run?"

Jane began to struggle again, but this was futile against Daniel's strength. "Make 'im turn me loose," she wailed.

"I think I'll hang on to you a bit," Daniel replied cheerfully.

Jane glared at me. "Are you a procuress? And here I thought you was pure as the driven snow."

"Certainly not." My tone was stern. "I am neither of those things."

"Then why won't you let me go? It ain't your business, and I can be well away."

"If the sergeant and inspector take it into their heads that you're guilty, they'll hunt for you across London and not stop until they find you," I said. "You'll never work again, and you'll endanger any family or friends you run to."

Jane stilled, as though she hadn't considered this. That she hesitated to endanger loved ones raised her in my estimation.

"Tell *me*, at least, why you ran," I went on. "We'll decide what the sergeant needs to know."

Jane's eyes widened. "You wouldn't peach?"

"That rather depends. Have you been pinching things from the house?"

"No." Her quick outrage made me believe her. "I ain't a fool. I'd get the noose for that."

"Then why?"

Jane went quiet in Daniel's grip, though he was experienced enough not to release her. "I think her ladyship killed him," Jane said mournfully. "Only, I don't blame her, like. His young lordship was always so awful to her. I don't want to say nuffink that will get her into trouble."

I listened in surprise. I hadn't thought Jane an admirer of Lady Babcock, though when I thought it through, she'd been more dismissive of Lord Babcock and his first wife. It had been Mrs. Morgan who'd told me the second Lady Babcock had been no better than a tart, and Mary who'd derided her.

"Why do you say this?" I asked Jane. "Except for the fact that Lord Alfred was rude to his stepmother, there must be another reason you suppose it."

Jane cast a sidelong glance at Daniel. "Is this the Mr. McAdam you were talking about? The one you sent Tess out to find this morning?"

That she'd deduced this made my respect for her rise even more.

"At your service," Daniel said in his most congenial tone. "You can tell us anything, Jane. We're good at keeping things confidential."

"You talk funny for a tramp," Jane declared, then she heaved a resigned sigh. "All right, I'll tell you. Her ladyship and Cook have been arguing back and forth all week, going into corners and speaking sharply, arms waving. I caught sight of her ladyship with Mrs. Morgan in the larder, and her ladyship *never* comes below stairs. Mrs. Morgan went upstairs a time or two as well, which ain't usual. I expected Mrs. Morgan to get the sack any day, but then she grows powerful sick. And now ..." Jane's voice grew thick with tears. "I ain't staying in a house where the family murders each other and poisons the staff."

I could not argue this last point. "If you believe her ladyship did these things, why do you not want to tell the police?"

"'Cause she's been kind to me, hasn't she?" Jane turned to me pleadingly. "She made old Seabrook hire me, when I didn't have nowhere to go. Her ladyship caught me shivering on the street steps and told me to go into the kitchen, eat something, and then help out a while. That were about a year ago—I been here ever since. Seabrook tells us not to speak poorly of her ladyship, but she don't like her, that's certain. I had to pretend I felt the same, in spite of her ladyship's charity to me, so I could keep on Seabrook's good side." She sagged. "I try not to talk about her at all."

An interesting tale. It sounded as though Lady Babcock indeed had a kind heart beneath her vacant expression. Even if Lady Babcock had not, in fact, laced the tea with morphine, she'd been concerned enough about her cook, despite their quarrels, to look in on her.

I was impressed that Lady Babcock had retained her compassion after she'd been thrust into her husband's family and lived for years surrounded by people who didn't like her.

Would a person who took pity on a girl in the street murder her husband's beloved son? As far as I knew, Lady Babcock had no children, so she wouldn't be clearing Lord Alfred out of the way so her own son could inherit. She also didn't sound like a lady who would lash out in a pique.

"It seems unlikely Lady Babcock stabbed him," I told Jane. "She and Mrs. Morgan could have been arguing about what to serve for Easter dinner, which has nothing to do with the murder."

I didn't quite believe that, but I needed to reassure Jane.

"Suppose," she conceded.

"Sergeant Scott only wishes to know where you were when the murder occurred. You were helping me in the kitchen. Tess and I had eyes on you the entire time. That is all you need to tell him."

"Mary nipped out for a bit," Jane said unhappily.

I came alert, as did Daniel. "Pardon?" I asked.

"After we sent up the fish and were in a bother about getting the ham and its fixings ready at the same time. I saw Mary slip out the back door and go up the outside stairs."

Had she? I'd never noticed, but we'd been focused on the meal, and Mary had been elbow-deep in her sink, or so I'd believed.

"She was back down when Mrs. Seabrook announced his lordship's death," I recalled.

Mary had been more outraged than the rest of us when Mrs. Seabrook had told us the meal was off. Had Mary already known *why* it was, her reaction feigned?

Mary had professed great admiration for Lord Alfred. Had she been madly in love with the young man? If he'd rebuffed her, and she'd been upset ... Oh, dear heavens.

"I will speak with Mary," I said firmly. "Jane, you go back inside, tell Sergeant Scott when he calls for you exactly where you were before Lord Alfred was found, and remain silent about everything else."

"I know how to keep mum," Jane declared. "I only told you, because you and your man pried it out of me. I was afraid the Peeler would too."

"You've confessed it to us, so your conscious is clear. Now, return before Sergeant Scott decides you've run away and sends constables out to find you."

Jane nodded, as though agreeing to be sensible. Daniel finally let her go, and she walked away from us, squaring her shoulders as she went.

I kept a sharp eye on her, but she made for Portman Square without breaking stride. I'd be right behind her as soon as I finished speaking with Daniel.

I turned to him, my resolve cracking. "Please tell me Lord Alfred had so many enemies that anyone in London could have broken in and killed him in his own front hall. I don't like to think someone who lives in the house did it, even though I know it's most likely."

"He seems to have been a well-liked young man about Town." Daniel dashed my hopes for an easy solution. "His father, on the other hand, is a stern taskmaster and has made many political enemies. It is possible one of them decided to rid him of his heir to take their vengeance, but improbable they'd do it in such a haphazard way."

"Lord Babcock wouldn't invite his enemies to dine in

his home with his family, would he?" I mused. "Lady Cynthia described the guests, who seem innocuous enough. Though I suppose one never knows."

"Unfortunately, true." Daniel scanned the street, as though watching for any observers. "Cheer up. The police might conclude that someone in passing realized the front door was unguarded, entered to rob the place, encountered Lord Alfred in the hall, stabbed him, and fled. It is plausible."

I also preferred that solution, but something in my bones told me it wasn't true. "If the police dismiss the murder as a burglary gone wrong, when it wasn't, then others in the house might be in danger. Lady Babcock herself."

I pondered anew Mrs. Morgan's admonition to me about Lady Babcock. *Watch out for her.*

Instead of a warning against the lady, could it have been a plea? *Watch out for those trying to harm her.* I truly needed to speak to Mrs. Morgan again.

"Daniel, when you were worried about me going to Portman Square, why?" I asked abruptly. "Did you believe something bad would happen at that house?"

"No." The word was spoken forthrightly. "I'd have done everything in my power to prevent you entering Lord Babcock's abode if I'd thought a murder would occur there. But, as you've no doubt concluded, I've had business in this square before. One of Lord Babcock's neighbors knows who I really am. Well, one of my personas while working for Monaghan, I mean."

Daniel finished wistfully. *Who I really am.* He didn't know, not for certain.

I wanted to take Daniel into my arms there and then and tell him it didn't matter. He was himself, and that was enough for me.

However, we stood on a public street near the happy families of Portman Square, with me in my work dress and Daniel garbed as an unsavory vagabond.

"Is that why you are in your current guise?" I asked. "Instead of off having Easter dinner with your son?"

Daniel huffed a laugh. "I couldn't watch over you if Lord Babcock's neighbor recognized me as the rather annoying secretary he'd employed last year. Also, James is lurking too, but he's better than me at being unobserved. He insisted on helping." His expression held forbearance.

"Oh." I darted my gaze about but saw no one who resembled the tall James. "Well, tell him he has become quite skilled."

"Nothing that should worry a father," Daniel said tightly.

James was a good lad, I knew. He'd take care of himself, and Daniel too.

"Speaking of fathers," I continued. "Do you know if there is any truth to the rumor that Lord Alfred wasn't Lord Babcock's son?"

Daniel shook his head. "Probably not. From what I understand, Lord Babcock and his first wife were a devoted couple. The first Lady Babcock bore Lord Alfred several years into the marriage, so he cannot have been the product of a liaison before their engagement. I believe the first Lady Babcock gained her reputation for promiscuity because she had many offers to wed in her youth. She turned them all down to choose Lord

Babcock, who was fifteen years her senior and a respectable marquess to boot. The younger gentlemen were jealously enraged, the young ladies who'd hoped to land themselves a lordship were furious, and so the rumors began."

"Despicable," I said in disgust. "Because the woman found someone she liked better than the twits who fluttered about her?" I'd seen similar young bucks flirt determinedly with Cynthia because her father had a title, as well as young lady debutants sneer at her for being unmarried still.

I tamped down my outrage to return to our problem. "How do you know all this?" I asked Daniel. "Do you have a dossier on every family in Mayfair?"

"The neighbor. When I was with him in my capacity as a snobbish secretary, he gossiped at length about everyone he knew."

Daniel would have tucked away these bits and pieces of information in case they came in handy with an investigation later. That, and he was simply interested in people.

I reluctantly stepped away from Daniel, resigning myself to the reality of the day. "Well, I must return and make certain Jane speaks to the inspector, and then visit Mrs. Morgan."

Daniel put a hand on my arm. "Take care," he said in a low voice. "Someone in that house is not averse to sliding a knife into whomever they wish. I'd rather you and Tess returned home and let McGregor and Sergeant Scott handle things."

"I will, once the person is arrested and taken away," I

promised. "I don't like to leave Jane and Mary to the machinations of the police."

"You have no obligation to either of those young women," Daniel pointed out.

"Why does that matter? If there is danger in Lord Babcock's home, I can't callously abandon them to it."

Daniel's smile told me he liked my answer. "I will be nearby, if you need to shout for me. As I say, so is James."

"I will be careful, I promise you." I should turn away now and hurry back to the house, but I hesitated. "I wish ..."

"Yes?" Daniel asked with interest. "What do you wish, Kat?"

His voice had grown quieter, and the space between us decreased.

What I wished was to go home with him, to have the only Easter dinner I cooked be one for him, James, and Grace. To have my own life instead of dedicating all my time to those who little appreciated it.

I let out a breath. "Never mind. No use pining for castles in the air."

Daniel's hands closed around mine and squeezed them. I thought he would speak, give me hope for such a future, but in the end, he only flashed me his warm smile, released me, and faded into the shadow of the fence.

I made myself turn and leave him, squaring my shoulders as Jane had done, and walked back to the house in Portman Square.

———

I WANTED to speak to Mary first thing upon my return and question her about leaving her post, but I did not see Mary at her sink.

"She's in with the sergeant," Tess informed me. "Jane's next."

Jane was busily spooning cooked vegetables into bowls to be covered with cheesecloth and stored in the larder for later consumption. She glanced up at me when Tess spoke her name but remained silent. She looked more at ease, though, and I hoped I'd reassured her somewhat.

For now, I prepared several pots of tea and a large platter of pastries I'd meant for the Easter dinner. The ladies of the house would be upset with the arrival of the police, and tea and pastries might soothe them. I made a smaller pot and plate for Mrs. Morgan and asked Tess to help me carry it all upstairs.

Before we could leave, Mary banged out of the housekeeper's parlor and dashed into the kitchen, tears smeared on her face.

"I never," she sobbed. "I never killed him. I loved him. *Tell* him, Mrs. Holloway."

CHAPTER 9

$\mathcal{I}$ stepped out of the kitchen to find Sergeant Scott at the door of the housekeeper's parlor, a look of resignation on his face. He made no move to pursue Mary or make an arrest.

"Send in the other kitchen maid," the sergeant instructed me, then disappeared back into the room.

Jane, her face wan, quietly moved around me and down the hall. She rapped once on the door, then entered, her body stiff.

I returned to the kitchen once Jane was safely inside. I knew Sergeant Scott would not let me in there with her, and I only hoped my admonition to be sensible and say little helped her.

"Sit down, Mary," I told the weeping girl. I fetched another teacup, poured the hot beverage into it, and set the cup on the table next to her. "You were wrong to run upstairs when we were so busy, but you did, and there's no use breaking down over it. If Sergeant Scott believed you'd gone up to murder the young master, he'd have arrested you on the spot."

"I didn't," Mary wailed. "I just wanted to catch sight of him, like."

"Of course you did." I remained firm but put some sympathy in my tone. "The important point, Mary, is whether you saw anyone else when you were hoping for a glimpse of Lord Alfred."

"I never did see him." Mary sniffled. "Saw everyone else milling about, drifting to the dining room, but not his young lordship."

"When you say *everyone else*, who do you mean, exactly?"

"His sister and stepmum, with their stepmum's aunt." Mary pulled a handkerchief from her pocket and swiped at her nose. "His dad and cousin. Your ladyship friend and her beau. They took their time going in, chattering to one another as they wandered down the hall. The rest was already in the dining room. Mrs. Seabrook was there too, clearing up the drawing room behind them. I was ever so afraid she'd see me."

"What about Lord Alfred?" I asked. "Had he gone into the dining room? Or back into the drawing room? Perhaps he spoke with Mrs. Seabrook?"

Mary shook her head vehemently. "I told you, I never saw him. Don't know where he was."

This was interesting. If Lord Alfred hadn't been with either the group in the dining room or those in the hall, where had he been? And why?

"Did you tell Sergeant Scott this?" I asked.

Mary nodded. "He made me go over it and over it, but I know he thought I did it." Her sobs renewed.

I had not imagined the weariness in Sergeant Scott's expression when he'd watched Mary run to the kitchen. Her histrionics must have worn down even his stoicism.

"Have a cake and drink that tea," I ordered. "You will feel better. Then continue putting away the food. Tess, help me with the trays."

My crisp instructions cut through Mary's weeping. She nodded and obediently lifted the teacup to her lips.

Tess rolled her eyes behind Mary's back but seized the heaviest tray and moved off toward the backstairs. I picked up the second tray and followed her.

When we reached the main floor, we found the house very quiet. The dining room and drawing room doors were both closed, Inspector McGregor presumably interviewing the guests behind one of them.

I asked a footman, who was now diligently watching the front door, where the ladies of the household were. He regarded me sullenly and pointed upward with a stiff finger. I sent him a sharp frown then bade Tess continue up the main stairs.

The large first floor held only a sitting room and a library, so on we went to the next floor, where the mistress's boudoir was likely to be. A maid who was nipping from bedroom to bedroom, linens in her hands, guided us to Lady Babcock's chamber.

"Thank you," I said to the maid.

She paused to whisper to me. "The breakfast you cooked for us was ever so nice. Wish you could stay here."

I nodded at her compliment, though all I wanted to do

after this day was return to my familiar demesne of Mount Street.

The maid opened the door for us, and Tess and I strode inside with our burdens.

Lady Cynthia rose from a settee she shared with the young woman I assumed was Lady Margaret, the deceased's man's sister. Lady Babcock sat on a chair at her dressing table, removed from them, wearing a bewildered expression.

An older woman with a thin face and graying hair reposed on a delicate chair in the corner near the window, as though not wanting to be noticed. I deduced she was Miss Jordan, Lady Babcock's aunt.

Miss Jordan flashed a look at me as I entered that told me she saw more than her passive way of carrying herself indicated.

Mrs. Bywater, fortunately, was absent. She was not the sort of person one wanted close when needing comfort.

"I brought a repast, your ladyship," I said when no one spoke.

I set the smaller tray on a table near the door and moved to help Tess with the large one, which we placed on the low table in front of the settee. Cynthia seated herself again and immediately began dispensing tea, as neither Lady Babcock nor Lady Margaret seemed able to take on the task.

Lady Margaret's eyes were red-rimmed, her face blotchy. I noted that she smelled strongly of a floral perfume, possibly donned to entice her cousin Desmond, or perhaps it was something she wore for supper every day. Lady Cynthia never wore scent, not liking to smell like a chemist's shop, she always jested.

"I don't want anything," Lady Margaret declared tearfully. "Take it all away."

"Nonsense." Cynthia finished pouring a cup and shoved it at Lady Margaret. "Best thing for shock is to take nourishment. Else you'll waste away."

As Lady Margaret possessed the artificial slenderness so popular these days, it wouldn't take much for her to fade to nothing.

Lady Magaret grasped the teacup and saucer, either because she agreed with Cynthia or because Cynthia was a stubborn force.

I pushed the plate of pastries toward them. I'd worked hard on these, laminating the dough and brushing some with jam, others with chocolate and hazelnut cream.

Cynthia took up a jam pastry and bit off a large chunk while Lady Margaret regarded them listlessly.

"Perfect," Cynthia stated after she chewed and swallowed. "Mrs. Holloway has a fine touch."

I nodded my thanks as I fixed a cup of tea and carried it to Lady Babcock. "I've put a bit of sugar in this and a dollop of cream," I told her as I held it out to her. "It will fortify you nicely."

Lady Babcock took the cup, gazing at me as though she'd never seen me or anyone else in the room before. Of the three ladies, she seemed the most dazed.

"What has happened in my house?" Lady Babcock murmured to me, so softly I barely caught it.

I bent closer. "Lord Alfred's death is a terrible thing,

your ladyship, I know. We can only let ourselves grieve and then carry on."

This is what I'd told myself after my mother had died. The words sounded as hollow now as they had then. I'd been fortunate to have Joanna to hug me until my weeping ceased, and not much longer after that, I'd borne Grace. Grace had done much to return happiness to my life.

"They don't want me to carry on," Lady Babcock said to me, *sotto voce*. "They want me to hang for murdering Alfred."

I could not say, *Of course, they don't*, because it had been made clear that most in this household did not want her here.

Would Lord Babcock's lofty position protect Lady Babcock if she was accused? I dimly recalled some law or other from the past that said a husband was responsible for his wife's wrongdoings, but I wasn't certain if that was still the case.

The law might, at the very least, have Lady Babcock put into an asylum for the insane—one of those remote country places with thick walls and strong gates. Lady Margaret and the servants might be pleased by that outcome.

The question was, would any of them go so far as to sacrifice Lord Alfred to rid themselves of Lady Babcock? The idea seemed far-fetched. It was more likely that Lady Babcock's enemies would take advantage of the situation to try to pin the crime on her.

That left the problem of who had actually crept up behind Lord Alfred and stabbed him.

"All will be well," I said softly to Lady Babcock. "Drink your tea."

She lifted the cup to her lips and took a long swallow. That she did so without hesitation, made me believe she hadn't, in fact, dosed Mrs. Morgan's tea. Lady Babcock would be more suspicious of a cup I handed her if she was used to manipulating people with dollops of morphine.

Once Lady Babcock seemed calmer, I carried tea to Miss Jordan. She took it with murmured thanks.

"Will you look out for her?" I whispered.

"Of course," Miss Jordan said stoutly.

A dragon, I decided. One in simple gray broadcloth.

Would *she* have killed the son of the house to protect Lady Babcock from him? Perhaps Lord Alfred had gone beyond rudeness and had dealt the occasional blow to his disliked stepmother—it was not unheard of. Miss Jordan might have decided he needed to be taken from Lady Babcock's life. An idea worth pondering.

Miss Jordan began sipping her tea, ignoring me, and I returned to the others. Tess had quietly served Lady Margaret some of the cakes, though the young woman only stared at the plate on the table.

I signaled to Tess that we should leave. Tess curtsied to the room, eyes down, as though she was the most obedient maid in the history of maids. I lifted the tray I'd prepared for Mrs. Morgan, and Tess followed me out.

"Whew, I don't envy our Lady Cynthia staying in there," Tess murmured to me as we reached the door to the back stairs.

"Neither do I," I agreed as Tess opened the door for

me. "Back to the kitchen for you, Tess. And thank you. On a cheerful note, we should be home soon."

"That's the truth." Tess grinned at me and then clattered down the stairs while I ascended them.

I found Mrs. Morgan sitting up in her bed, looking much better. She'd obviously drunk no more morphine-laced tea today.

"Ever so kind," Mrs. Morgan said as I laid the tray on her bedside table. "What with all the goings-on here, I think I'll give me notice."

"Perhaps that would be for the best." I poured out a cup of tea, added a bit of sugar, and handed it to her.

Mrs. Morgan's eyes narrowed, though she readily took the cup. "Are you after my post, Mrs. Holloway?"

"No, indeed." I'd have to be desperate to work for this family, I decided. "I only meant you might be happier elsewhere."

"Could be. Course, if I leave, her ladyship will be thrown to the wolves."

"You are afraid *for* her." I'd finally settled on that interpretation of what she'd been trying to tell me before.

Mrs. Morgan took a noisy sip of tea. "Even her own husband can't be bothered with her most of the time. Besotted at first, because she was once so lovely, but she don't have much in the way of good sense. A man gets weary of that, don't he?"

It occurred to me that in his time of loss, Lord Babcock hadn't wanted his wife next to him. He might have ordered her to withdraw to her chamber with Lady Margaret and Cynthia, or perhaps it had been Cynthia's suggestion.

"I don't believe she killed Lord Alfred," I said.

"Eh? Of course she didn't. Her ladyship don't have that sort of cunning. I tried to tell her to be careful in this house, what with how the family treats her, especially with young Desmond arriving."

Third Cousin Desmond, whom Cynthia had told me about. "Would Cousin Desmond risk murdering Lord Alfred?" I wondered out loud. "His brother, Stephan, is the one who will inherit." So Cynthia had indicated. "Does he dote on his brother so much that he'd sacrifice himself to ensure Stephan is the next marquess?"

Mrs. Morgan snorted a laugh. "Not young Desmond, that scrawny nuisance. I've known him since he was in short pants, and believe me, he has no love for his older brother. No, if he offed Lord Alfred, it would be in a fit of pique alone. Young Alfred used to poke fun at him something awful, and young Desmond was always a bit sensitive."

"Lady Margaret wants to marry him?" I'd have thought the pampered young woman I'd observed downstairs would prefer a handsome, brawny, and very wealthy man to be her husband. Wouldn't hurt if he was already a duke or some such.

"Those two have been thick as thieves since they were children. Lady Babcock believes Lady Margaret ought to marry a quiet man and go live in the country somewhere, instead of larking about the metropolis with her friends. Girls these days are bold as brass, ain't they?"

Lady Margaret had seemed more lethargic than bold, but then, she'd suffered a shock from the loss of her brother this day. Her face had betrayed her weeping. Perhaps she ought to marry Desmond after all and try to find some happiness.

"Mark my words," Mrs. Morgan went on darkly. "It were Seabrook what killed him, if it were anyone."

I started. "Why do you say that?"

Mrs. Morgan shrugged. "She never liked Lord Alfred. Lord Alfred always ragged on her, just as he did to his stepmother. Lord Alfred was a cruel young man to his own family. Outside it, butter wouldn't melt in his mouth, as they say. Had much of polite society wrapped around his finger."

I'd already wondered whether Mrs. Seabrook, upstairs in the drawing room once the diners had departed it, had done the deed, for whatever reason. She was a robust woman.

Other ideas poured through my head, distracting me as I nodded at Mrs. Morgan. "No doubt the police will find the culprit."

"Those fools? Ha. Couldn't find a piece of hay in a haystack." Mrs. Morgan slurped her tea noisily and reached for the pastry.

"I'll leave you to it," I said, as Mrs. Morgan had fixed her attention on her repast. "I'm sure your kitchen maids will be happy to have you back again."

Another snort told me what Mrs. Morgan thought of my platitudes.

I departed as she masticated the pastry, and descended once more below stairs.

———

By the time I reached the kitchen, Tess and Mary had made good headway on packing up our things. Jane was less downcast though still tense.

"The sergeant were ever so polite," Jane told me, sounding reluctant to admit it. "It was like you said, Mrs. H. He only wanted to know where I was at half past one, when we was sending the meal upstairs. He didn't want me to tell him anything else."

I did not know Sergeant Scott well, but he seemed to me a practical man. He wouldn't be interested in Jane's past if it wasn't relevant. The sergeant could be as intimidating as the growling and grumbling Inspector McGregor, though in a cool way I found a bit more frightening than the inspector's bluster. However, Sergeant Scott had proved his pragmatism in my last encounter with him.

As we continued the work, I heard a familiar click of heels in the passageway, heralding the arrival of Mrs. Bywater. She gazed about the room when she arrived, focusing on the foodstuffs still waiting to be put into their crates.

"Leave nothing behind," she admonished me. "All these vegetables, all these potatoes. They should already have been packed."

"Not those." I shielded a basket of leftover produce. "I purchased them for *this* house."

"Did you?" Mrs. Bywater widened her eyes. "Then they come with us. Lord Rankin will reimburse you through your wages."

"I put them on the marquess's account, ma'am." I bobbed a shallow curtsey as though I was in awe of saying the word *marquess*.

"Oh, well, in that case." Mrs. Bywater backed away from the argument. "Be sure to pack what is ours, including what you've already cooked. We can dine on that for a few days. And all of the wine. Close up those crates, Tess, before someone takes anything."

Mrs. Bywater shot a quick glance at Mary and Jane, as though certain they'd pinch the leftovers and rush out into the street with them. Mary regarded her fearfully, Jane with a scowl.

"All our things will go back to Mount Street, I assure you," I said in soothing tones.

"See that they do. I'll visit the larder this evening and check, so no giving things away or eating them yourselves."

"Of course, ma'am." I gave her another curtsey.

Mrs. Bywater's eyes narrowed at my sudden docility, but she changed the subject.

"Leave out a loaf of bread and some butter," she instructed me. "So that Lady Babcock and her husband will have something to eat. I adore Lady Babcock—so generous to our little charitable society—but she is apt to forget simple things like nourishing herself."

I had the feeling that if the family wished to eat at all, they'd need more sustenance than bread and butter.

"Is his lordship all right?" I asked Mrs. Bywater. "Considering."

"Lord Babcock is made of stern stuff," Mrs. Bywater said decidedly. "He still has an heir, so all is not lost."

Jane blinked at this callous statement, but she quickly dropped her gaze and helped Tess nail the crates shut.

Mrs. Bywater winced as Tess gave her crate a hard

blow with a hammer. Mrs. Bywater sniffed, looked over the kitchen once more, and thankfully took herself away.

"I was right," Jane said once we heard Mrs. Bywater retreat and the backstairs door slam. "She *is* a cow."

"Enough," I told her, but gently. "I will run out and see if we have a cart to tote this home in."

I headed up the stairs, not bothering with a coat. The spring day had become even warmer, and I perspired as I hurried to the road where I'd last seen Daniel. I hoped he'd lend his delivery wagon, as no other was in sight. Apparently, Mrs. Bywater hadn't thought through how we'd lug all these things back.

Daniel was no longer at the railings where I'd left him. As I paused, contemplating where he might have gone, James spoke behind me.

"He's gone."

I spun around, my hand to my heart. "Good heavens, James. You do like to spring from nowhere."

"Sorry, Mrs. H.," James shot me a lopsided grin that was so like his father's. "Dad went off to assist Inspector McGregor. The inspector's decided to arrest the murdered man's cousin for doing the deed, and the cousin is cutting up rough."

"Third Cousin Desmond?" I asked in astonishment. "No, that is all wrong."

I hadn't heard any shouting or seen Inspector McGregor bundling Cousin Desmond out into the street, but we'd been hastening to pack under Mrs. Bywater's admonishments, Tess enjoying making a racket with the hammer.

James shrugged. "Right or wrong, they're hauling him to the magistrate. Dad had to help the constables hold on to him. They're trundling him off, even as we speak."

CHAPTER 10

"Third Cousin Desmond did not kill Lord Alfred," I declared.

"Do you want to run after them?" James asked. "Tell Inspector McGregor?"

I nearly did let myself chase whatever police wagon had taken away Cousin Desmond, but I stopped. Neither Inspector McGregor nor a magistrate would be interested in my thoughts at this moment, and I had no evidence that could clear Cousin Desmon's name. My idea that he couldn't have done it would be dismissed.

No, sensitive Desmond might have to spend a night in Bow Street or even Newgate, though Lord Babcock, if he could, would prevent that.

Desmond was now second in line for the marquessate. If he disliked his older brother as much as Mrs. Morgan said he did, he might not, in theory, stop at anything to become the marquess himself. A magistrate and a high court judge might believe that.

"No," I said. "I will have to do this another way. Any

chance your dad's delivery wagon is about? I must trundle all our goods back to Mount Street. The sooner, the better, I think."

James touched his cap. "Right away, Mrs. H."

He sprang away with the enthusiasm of youth, leaving me pondering as I walked back to the Babcock house.

The news of Desmond's arrest had reached the kitchen by the time I arrived.

"I never liked him," Mary said darkly. "He was always cruel to the young master. Calling him a bastard, and all."

Mrs. Morgan had said the opposite, that Lord Alfred had taunted Third Cousin Demond. I couldn't be certain which was the truth. A bit of both, I supposed.

If Cousin Desmond had believed the tale that Lord Alfred was illegitimate, that might make Desmond's motive to kill Lord Alfred even stronger in the eyes of the law. Lord Babcock had apparently been satisfied that Alfred had sprung from his seed, but rumor was a powerful thing.

Tess and I had nearly finished bundling away our things—I had no leisure to sit in a corner and ruminate—when Lady Cynthia entered the kitchen.

"Can you take another pot of tea to Margaret?" she asked. "She is beside herself now that her beloved Desmond's been arrested so quickly after she lost her brother."

Lady Cynthia spoke briskly, as though she was becoming rather fed up with the traumatic events in this house. She obviously pitied Lady Margaret, however. Hence the order of tea.

"Of course," I said. "Tell her not to worry. I don't believe her cousin did it."

Cynthia studied me in relief. "I'm happy to hear you say that. Margaret doesn't need more trouble. I don't think Desmond did it either. He's a bit of a weed."

"Perhaps you ought to go home now," I told her kindly. "There's not much more you can do."

"I'd love to, but I'll stay on." Cynthia heaved a resigned sigh. "McGregor dismissed the other guests, who have all fled. Lord Babcock has shut himself into his study, not wanting to see anyone but his valet. Auntie is already storming home. Apparently, she is annoyed she was in a house where a murder was committed and has no intention of staying any longer."

As Mrs. Bywater could be trying on her best days, I thought perhaps it was better for Lord Babcock's family if she went.

"I'll have the tea ready in a trice and bring it up," I told Cynthia, then leaned to whisper to her. "Make certain no one eats or drinks anything I haven't prepared, and eat nothing that has been left unattended for even a moment."

Cynthia's eyes went wide. "Do you think the poisoner will strike again? Do they mean to kill everyone in the house?"

"We can sincerely hope not. But please monitor the food and drink after I'm gone."

"That I will. Good Lord."

"Thank you." I returned to my usual tones. "Have you seen Mrs. Seabrook at all?" The housekeeper had been notably absent since announcing Lord Alfred's death.

"She's rushing about, clucking, because the upstairs

rooms have been left in such a state. She's busy chivvying the maids to put them to rights."

I imagined Mrs. Seabrook gave orders like a general in battle. "Up you go. I'll bring the tray."

"You are too good for us, Mrs. H."

I accepted the compliment with modesty, as usual. Cynthia grinned at me then took herself away.

James thumped down the outside stairs and knocked on the door to announce the cart was ready. Tess brightened when she saw him, and Jane and Mary did as well, though for different reasons. The kitchen maids were no doubt noting that James was quite handsome.

"My, my," Mary said after James had hefted a few crates outside. "Ain't he a one?"

Her tone was admiring, which told me her attachment to Lord Alfred had been little more than a passing infatuation.

Jane said nothing at all, but the way her gaze fixed on James showed genuine interest. James was a free spirit, I wanted to tell them, not ready to walk out with a young lady, but I held my tongue. Let them have this one refreshing moment in a bleak day.

While Tess continued to supervise the packing, I prepared a fresh pot of tea, added pastries that would not survive the journey back to Mount Street, and once more ascended through the house. When I paused on the first floor, I saw Mrs. Seabrook issuing stentorian commands to two maids who rushed about, trying to obey her.

Lady Babcock, Miss Jordan, Cynthia, and Lady Magaret had remained in Lady Babcock's chamber.

Lady Margaret was crying fresh tears, wiping them

copiously on an already wet handkerchief. Her eyes were redder than before, and she morosely regarded the tea I set before her.

When I carried tea to Lady Babcock, she gazed up at me with more resolution than she'd had when I'd left her.

"I've made up my mind," she said quietly. "I'm going to live with my aunt for a bit. She needs looking after, and I will welcome the change."

"Perhaps that is the best thing, your ladyship," I agreed.

I was not horrified or disapproving that she'd abandon her husband while he grieved for his son. If Lord Babcock had wanted her comfort, she'd already be shut in the study with him.

I had the feeling I was witnessing the shattering of a marriage. The Babcocks might not shock the world with a divorce, but I wagered they'd begin living separate lives. It was too bad, but I'd experienced a difficult marriage myself, and being on one's own was infinitely preferable to that.

Cynthia encouraged Lady Margaret to sip some tea. Margaret coughed as it went down, but she managed to swallow then fell limply against the settee's pillows once more.

I sent Cynthia an inquiring glance, wondering if she needed me to stay, but Cynthia nodded for me to go.

I hoped she'd persuade Lady Margaret to bed and to take something to make her sleep, though not the morphine that was floating about this house. I wondered if Sergeant Scott would search for it, or if he and Inspector McGregor would be satisfied that they'd caught the killer and not bother.

Desmond couldn't possibly have laced Mrs. Morgan's tea, I was certain. He hadn't arrived at the house until shortly before dinner was served today.

Why Mrs. Morgan's tea had been dosed was still a mystery. Had Mrs. Morgan guessed that Lord Alfred would be murdered, and the murderer wanted to shut her up? But if so, Mrs. Morgan could have passed that information on, either to me when I'd taken her the broth, or later, when she'd felt better.

The effect of Mrs. Morgan's illness was that she hadn't been in the kitchen. The morphine might have been intended to make certain she stayed abed.

Had the person thought to poison Lord Alfred and blame the kitchen staff, or whoever took over for Mrs. Morgan, for serving him bad food? Was Mrs. Morgan the sort of cook who'd never let anyone near her dishes?

If so, the poisoner must have been dismayed at my diligence. I too let no one near the food except those I trusted, and as I'd told Mrs. Seabrook, I tasted everything myself.

Was that why they'd risked stabbing Lord Alfred?

In any case, Third Cousin Desmond had not been here to dollop morphine into Mrs. Morgan's tea.

That left Mrs. Seabrook, Lady Babcock, Lord Babcock, Lady Margaret, Alfred himself, Armitage, and the maids and footmen. I'd think only a physician would be able to get hold of morphine, but I acknowledged that anything could be stolen from anywhere.

I gave Lady Babcock and Miss Jordan one last glance of reassurance and left the room, breathing a sigh of relief when I closed the door behind me. Cynthia would guard the ladies well. I told myself there would be no more murder or attempted murder if we all remained diligent.

By the time I reached the kitchen once more, James and the three maids had finished loading the cart. I snatched up my coat and hat and ascended the outside stairs to find Tess climbing to the seat next to James for the ride home.

Mary leaned on the railings, gazing at James, her expression forlorn.

Jane faced me belligerently. "If ye had any heart, ye wouldn't go."

I regarded her with surprise. "My dear Jane, this house already has a cook. I cannot remain where I'm not employed."

"Then take me with ya."

I felt sorry for her, but there was little I could offer. "Hiring another kitchen assistant is not up to me," I said gently. "But I can put in a word for you at my agency if you wish to seek a better place."

Jane considered this, then softened. "That'd be good of you. Thank you, Mrs. Holloway."

"Not at all. Now, look in on Mrs. Morgan and make sure she gets well. Also, if Lady Cynthia asks you to help prepare food or drink this afternoon and evening, do your best to assist her."

Jane looked mystified at this request, but she nodded. The next moment, she amazed me by throwing her arms around me. "I'm so glad you came."

I returned her embrace, giving her an affectionate squeeze. "I'm glad I have as well."

Jane released me and self-consciously brushed tears from her eyes.

I definitely would request that my agency find Jane a much better place. She was skilled in the kitchen and shouldn't be held back. If I hadn't already had Tess, I'd have tried to persuade Mrs. Bywater to hire her.

As it was, I knew Mrs. Bywater would never agree to the expense of a second kitchen assistant, even if Lord Rankin was paying the bills. She'd have to write to Lord Rankin and explain, and I knew she feared annoying the titled man she was related to only through the marriage of her niece.

James gave us a cheery wave and started the cart down the street. Tess also waved her good-byes, the two maids returning them downheartedly.

As on the journey here, there was no room for me on the cart, so I chose to walk home. I bade the two maids farewell, vowing to look in on them from time to time. Jane nodded, but Mary burst into tears again as I turned away.

Once I crossed Oxford Street, I exhaled in relief. I saw James in his cart turn ahead of me, and I slowed my steps. I was in no hurry to unload the goods and then prepare the Bywaters a thrown-together supper to make up for their missed Easter feast. I was tired and out of sorts on this thoroughly rotten day.

James had pulled the cart to a halt in front of the house by the time I reached Mount Street, and Tess was scrambling to the ground. Without a word, James descended and started lugging the heaviest crates down into the kitchen. The lad was a blessing.

Mr. Davis waited for us below stairs, anxiously supervising James as he toted in the wine.

"I hope it hasn't been shaken up too much," Mr. Davis said worriedly. "Will ruin it, that will."

"We have been very careful," I told him as I hung up my coat and hat. "Do count and make certain they are all there, Mr. Davis, except for the two I used for sauces. The butler to Lord Babcock tried to abscond with some."

Mr. Davis's mouth pinched. "Armitage, you mean. He's a nasty piece of work. Has nicked things in great houses the length and breadth of England. I will count with double care." Mr. Davis waved me off. "Thank you for bringing the wine back, though in what state, remains to be seen."

"Not at all, Mr. Davis."

I left him brooding over the bottles like a doting father and turned to assist Tess and Elsie, who'd left her scullery, to put everything away. Tess told Elsie what that had gone on in the Babcock household, Elsie listening with rounded eyes. Mr. Davis and Mrs. Redfern, as well as the footmen, paused to listen, but I silently got on with preparing supper for the family.

I reflected on it all as I worked, shutting out the voices around me.

I could not make the pieces of the puzzle fit, and that annoyed me. The poisoning and the stabbing, regardless of what I'd speculated earlier, may or may not be connected. The antipathy for Lady Babcock, the question of Lord Alfred's legitimacy, Lord Babcock withdrawing to his study, and Mrs. Morgan's warnings might all be smoke.

However, as Inspector McGregor constantly pointed out to me, it was the business of the police to investigate and decide if they had enough evidence to charge someone with murder. In truth, none of this had anything to do with me.

And yet, I couldn't help wanting to protect the people in that house: Lady Babcock, who was out of her depth; Jane and Mary, who were innocent young women; Mrs. Morgan, who wasn't a bad sort; Lady Margaret in her intense grief. Even the brusque Mrs. Seabrook had my concern. She certainly could have committed both crimes, though I wasn't sure what she would gain by it.

I did consider that Mrs. Morgan herself could have done the murder. She could have dosed her own tea with an amount of morphine that wouldn't kill her in order to feign an illness, waited until the family and guests had gone into dinner, nipped down the backstairs, stabbed Lord Alfred, and scuttled again to her bed.

As in the case with Mrs. Seabrook, *why* Mrs. Morgan would do such a thing, I had no idea, although she'd proved to be as protective of Lady Babcock as Lady Babcock's aunt professed to be.

Of course, this idea would suppose Mrs. Morgan knew about morphine and how much to use on herself. Plus, she'd have to be swift, something her age and bulk might prohibit. In addition, she'd have to know that Lord Albert would linger in the hall after the others went into the dining room. He'd claimed an aching stomach—which could mean he too had been given something to make him hesitate instead of hurrying in with the others to eat a large meal.

I continued to speculate as we finished unpacking the foodstuffs and preparing the meal for the Bywaters, but I drew no definite conclusions. Mrs. Bywater did indeed visit the larder after supper, and she seemed disappointed she couldn't find fault with how I'd stored the leftovers.

Once she went upstairs again, we and the rest of the staff consumed our own suppers, and Tess, Elsie, and I cleaned up the subsequent mess.

I sent Tess to bed before long, as she was exhausted after our two extraordinary days. I remained in the kitchen after last of the staff had gone up, sitting at my familiar table and making notes in my book.

My hopes were that Daniel would come. I'd put aside some cold ham and a leftover bit of tart for him, but I had no idea if he'd have time to visit me. He might be assisting Inspector McGregor to determine whether Desmond had murdered his cousin Alfred.

I continued to write well past midnight, making scribbles in the margins when my thoughts wouldn't connect.

I realized after a while that I'd drawn a flower several times over. I halted my hand in surprise and stared down at it.

Of course, I thought, but I followed that with the words, *Make certain.*

I closed the notebook and rose, quietly moving down the passageway to the housekeeper's parlor. I had a key to it and unlocked the door.

The shelf in the corner held my three cookbooks. I flipped through one of them until I found its section on herbs and spices. I read the page I sought, my heart speeding.

I replaced the book on the shelf and returned to the kitchen in time to hear Daniel's knock on the back door. I quickly opened it, pulling him inside and embracing him with relief.

Daniel no longer wore an indigent person's garb but his own coat, homespun trousers, and thick cotton shirt. He also smelled nice, of the outdoors and coal smoke, nothing like the miasma that had clung to him with his disguise.

He returned my hug, pressing a kiss to my cheek. "That glad to see me, are you?"

I made myself release him. "I am always pleased to see you, Daniel, though I know you've only come for your Easter meal." Before he could answer my teasing, I drew him all the way inside and shut the door against the night.

"Let us sit and have tea," I said, towing him to the table. "And I will tell you who killed Lord Alfred."

CHAPTER 11

*D*aniel regarded me with a satisfying amount of surprise, his hand poised on the back of a chair. "You know?"

"I believe so," I amended. "Do sit down, please. Your hovering makes me nervous."

Daniel scraped the chair back and dropped into it obediently. "Do you plan to report your conclusions to Inspector McGregor?"

"I am reporting to *you*. I might be wrong, and I'd like your opinion before you make it known to Sergeant Scott or Inspector McGregor."

"I am agog to learn your solution." Daniel spoke lightly, but his expression held tension.

I took some time brewing tea and fetching the ham and rolls from the larder while Daniel watched me intently.

"That the police think it was done with a knife from the kitchen is interesting," I began as I sat next to Daniel and laid a fork and napkin near his plate. "It means the culprit had access to the kitchen, or to someone in the kitchen who could fetch the weapon for them. That person also would have to somehow obtain morphine."

Daniel lifted his fork. "You believe one person did both?"

"Yes, and I know why, although I don't know precisely how. Nor do I know the exact sequence of events. I can only guess them."

Daniel smiled as he scooped up a bite of ham. "Your guesses in the past have proved more accurate than those of the most thorough detectives I know."

"Very flattering," I admonished but good-naturedly.

I poured out the tea and proceeded to tell him all.

———

"The ladies will be down directly," Lady Cynthia said to me the next morning as she admitted me to the dining room of the Portman Square house.

I wasn't comfortable speaking to the family in the upstairs rooms, but Cynthia had wisely pointed out that Lady Babcock, Lady Margaret, and the marquess would be even more uncomfortable below stairs.

I could not, in good conscience, sit in an aristocrat's drawing room as though I were an honored guest—though I wore my best frock and hat, not my kitchen garb—but I acceded to the dining room as neutral territory. What I cooked ended up there, after all.

Mrs. Morgan was back in her kitchen, I learned upon

arrival, but she'd given her notice. So had Jane. In the meantime, Jane carried in a tray of tea things and a platter of cakes to nourish us.

Jane curtsied deferentially to Cynthia, gave me a nod with the hint of a smile, and disappeared again.

The gilded clock on the sideboard ticked monotonously a few more minutes before Mrs. Seabrook led the two ladies of the house into the room. Mrs. Seabrook wouldn't look at me, but her movements were stiff with disapproval. She likely blamed me for the cook and Jane giving notice, and she'd be correct.

Lady Margaret, dressed in a black silk gown that didn't fit her well—possibly quickly altered from something borrowed—kept her head bowed. Her unhappiness rolled from her, touching me palpably. She plunked herself in the chair at the foot of the table and gazed unseeingly out of the window.

Lady Babcock's dark frock, by contrast, had clearly been tailored for her, likely leftover from the last person she'd mourned. The cut had been in fashion only a few years ago, which meant her loss had been recent. My pity for her increased.

Cynthia poured tea for all as they got settled. Lady Babcock sat in a chair halfway along the table. Miss Jordan, still in the plain gray broadcloth frock I'd seen her in the day before, planted herself firmly in a chair by the sideboard, which put her almost directly behind Lady Babcock. The dragon was guarding her well.

Lord Babcock was the last to arrive. This was the first time I'd seen the man close to. He was tall and gaunt, his graying hair and lined face betraying his age. He also dressed in mourning, and his withdrawn manner touched my heart. It was obvious he had been grieving deeply. Whatever rumor surrounded Lord Alfred's origins, this man had cherished his son.

The way Lady Babcock followed her husband with her gaze as he passed her without a word told me she was still in love with Lord Babcock, despite his seeming indifference.

I wondered if Lady Babcock truly would go live with Miss Jordan for a bit, and what affect that would have on Lord Babcock.

"Thank you for coming down," Lady Cynthia said to the ladies and Lord Babcock as he took his place at the head of the table. "Mrs. Holloway had some news this morning. Your cousin Desmond will soon be released."

The reactions around the table were varied. Lord Babcock's thick brows shot upward, he clearly curious how a cook of all people would know such a thing, but I caught relief in his eyes.

A pucker appeared between Lady Babcock's brows, and Miss Jordan, if anything, looked angry.

Lady Margaret's reaction was the most dramatic of all. She burst into tears and collapsed forward onto the table. "Thank God," came her muffled words. "Thank God."

Mrs. Seabrook pulled smelling salts out of her pocket and hurried to Lady Margaret. Before she could reach the young woman, Lady Margaret sat up and wiped her eyes with an embroidered handkerchief. Mrs. Seabrook stepped back but kept the salts at the ready.

"Of course, he is not guilty," Lady Margaret declared,

her voice hoarse with weeping. "Never was. Didn't I tell you?"

"You did tell me," Lord Babcock rumbled gently. "Do not give way to hysteria, my dear. *You.*" His gentleness fell away as he pinned a stern gaze on me. "What do you mean by coming here and upsetting us? Why should the police tell *you* anything about our cousin?"

I had remained standing, knowing better than to sit at a table with an aristocrat and his family. I gave him a deferential curtsey. "I have friends who work for the police, your lordship. They decided the news would be best coming from Lady Cynthia and myself."

Lady Babcock raised her chin, her gaze alert. "Quite right," she said in her soft voice. "We've had enough of police in the house."

Miss Jordan agreed with a nod, though she said nothing. No one else in the room paid any attention to her.

Lady Margaret also did not speak, but her glance of intense dislike toward her stepmother told me she hoped the culprit would be Lady Babcock. How satisfying for her to watch Lady Babcock be shoved into a police wagon and taken away forever.

"I'll have Mrs. Holloway explain," Cynthia said. "She can relay it clearly. But I must say that I agree with the solution and so does Inspector McGregor. He will be along soon."

Lady Babcock's eyes widened. "Good heavens. Do you mean the killer is still here?" She sent a fearful gaze to the closed double door, as though the murderer would leap through it, brandishing a knife.

"Of course it is what she means," Lord Babcock

snapped at her, his eyes holding both rage and worry. "Carry on, Mrs. Holloway." His tone told me that I had better make his attendance at this tableau worth his while.

"Your ladyship," I said, speaking directly to Lady Babcock. "Has someone prescribed for you a packet of morphine powder? Or perhaps a liquid dose?"

Lady Babcock started. "Yes, indeed. My doctor. For my nerves. He told me to take only tiny bits at a time."

"Mrs. Morgan's dose was more than a tiny bit," I said. "It was enough to kill someone if they took the entire dollop. Thank heavens Mrs. Morgan did not." And *I* did not, I added to myself.

Mrs. Seabrook scowled at me. "Do you mean to accuse her ladyship of trying to poison Cook? You are highly impertinent, Mrs. Holloway."

"Not at all," I said quickly. "I am only pointing out that there was morphine in the house. Anyone who knew of it could have taken some to either harm the cook or at least lay her up for a while."

"Why should they?" Lord Babcock demanded.

It was quite unnerving for me to face Lord and Lady Babcock and tell them of the goings-on in their household. If Lord Babcock chose to be offended, he could have a word with Lord Rankin, and I might be out of a place in an instant. He could also spread the word to his cronies to tell their wives not to hire me.

I curled my fingers into my palms and forced myself to continue. They deserved the truth. And who knew who else might die before the killer's wild scheme was concluded?

"Mrs. Morgan suspected that there was danger in this

house," I told him. "I don't believe she knew exactly what would happen, but she knew *something* was wrong. She tried to warn Lady Babcock, but Lady Babcock did not want to believe her. These are the arguments the kitchen staff and Mrs. Seabrook witnessed. Mrs. Morgan confirmed this to me when I arrived today."

Lady Babcock gave me a faint nod. "She was right. I ought to have listened."

"At some point during the week, when Mrs. Morgan began to feel unwell—likely already being given the morphine—and the kitchen maids were preoccupied trying to carry on without her, the killer took the opportunity to pinch the kitchen knife that did the murder."

Miss Jordan made a soft sound of surprise, that again, no one else noticed.

Lady Margaret turned her gaze to her stepmother, waiting for me to denounce her. "How awful."

"All of you had access to the kitchen," I went on. "Mrs. Seabrook included, of course. It stands to reason, as this is your house. Lady Margaret went down from time to time to consult on dishes or to snatch a bite between meals, and lately, Lady Babcock went to continue her discussions with Mrs. Morgan. The only one who did not habitually go below stairs is your lordship."

Lord Babcock nodded once. "No reason for me to."

"The kitchen is a woman's domain, for the most part," I said. I did know some masterful male chefs, and I'd worked in a house where the husband had enjoyed cooking an omelet when he felt peckish, but in general my statement was correct.

"Her ladyship did come down quite often this past week," Mrs. Seabrook said in hushed tones.

"Mrs. Morgan is very protective of you, your ladyship." I gave Lady Babcock a polite nod. "It is good of her. She nearly died for that protection."

"What are you telling us?" Lord Babcock demanded. "That someone wanted to kill our cook as well as my son?"

His voice cracked on the last word, and I sent him a glance of sympathy. "Yes. I do not know if Mrs. Morgan suspected exactly what would happen, but the killer couldn't take the risk. If Mrs. Morgan grew ill or died, sickness or bad food could be blamed. She would also be out of the way for the Easter meal, which was when there would be opportunity to strike. With so many people in the house and the confusion between drawing room and dining room, there would be a chance to corner Lord Alfred alone. Perhaps he was also made to feel unwell so that he'd not rush in to dinner with the others. The open door could suggest an intruder, but if the police saw through that ruse, there would be plenty of other people in the house at the time who could be suspected. To Lady Margaret's regret, Mr. Desmond Charlton, of whom she is fond, was blamed."

Lady Margaret did not like me saying her name, but the corners of her lips softened. "At least dear Des has been proved innocent."

"It ought to have occurred to you that in the eyes of Detective Inspector McGregor, your cousin Desmond would have the strongest motive," I said. "He is now closer to inheriting the title and your father's wealth." I looked directly at Lady Margaret. "If you do marry Mr. Charlton, my lady, I will worry about the health of his older brother."

I heard intakes of breath around the room, and Lady Margaret stilled. "I beg your pardon? Are you accusing *me*?" She rose stiffly from her chair, her glare intense. "I'll have you sacked for implying such a thing, perhaps even arrested. Papa, do something about her."

"Let her speak." Lord Babcock's strong voice cut through his daughter's. Lady Margaret gaped at him, but she sank into her chair again, her cheeks scarlet.

I cleared my throat. "There is a flower—jasmine—that grows in warm climates but is cultivated in this country in hothouses. The blossoms are lovely and fragrant. Unfortunately for some people, they can cause a bad reaction, mostly itchy skin, and red, watery eyes. A person with this sensitivity could rub their face on the plant and make it appear as though they'd been weeping heavily."

"I *have* been weeping," Lady Margaret declared. "Why should I not be? My brother is dead and my beloved cousin was taken to the magistrate for it. I *do* have an arrangement of flowers in my bedchamber, which might include jasmine, but I am not sensitive to it at all."

"Yes, you are," Lord Babcock broke in. "Have been since you were a child, which is why I won't allow it in the house."

"I cannot help it if young men send me posies," Lady Margaret shot back.

"After your cousin was arrested, your tears were true," I resolutely went on. "But when I first served you tea, before that event, you smelled strongly of jasmine, I assumed from perfume or cologne, but your tears then were your reaction to the plant, not genuine grief. When it occurred to me that you'd given yourself only the appearance of grief, I had to wonder why. Perhaps you hadn't been close to your brother but wanted to show sorrow at his passing, even if you felt none, so that your father would not be upset. But it was more likely to disguise the fact that you were indeed happy he was gone. Cousin Desmond had little money, Lady Cynthia told me, and he wasn't approved of for you. But if Lord Alfred and Desmond's older brother were to die, the trifling matter of money would be solved." I dared look directly at Lord Babcock. "Possibly you might die as well, begging your pardon, your lordship."

What made me saddest of all was that Lord Babcock did not seem surprised. His mouth turned down, and he appeared to age before my eyes. "I was a fool to indulge and spoil you," he said heavily to Lady Margaret. "I've always known that."

Lady Margaret shoved her chair back and sprang to her feet once more. "You cannot possibly believe her," she announced to the rest of the room. "That I stabbed my own brother with a kitchen knife? That is madness. *She* was in the hall with him." Lady Margaret pointed a trembling finger at Lady Babcock. "*She* took Mrs. Morgan the tea with the morphine in it Saturday, giving *her* plenty of time to steal a knife." The pointing finger switched to me. "I'm sorry Mrs. Morgan fell ill, and we had to have *this* terrible cook work for us, but it was my stepmother that gave our cook the tea."

"I never said the morphine was in the tea," I said quietly. "Or on what day it was served."

Color seeped into Lady Margaret's face in red blotches. "Stop this!" she shrieked, balling her hands. "You cannot possibly take the word of a *cook* over mine."

"Sit down." Again, Lord Babcock's voice rolled over his daughter's. "I worried it was you from the first, which is why I did not want the police here." He turned to Cynthia with a hint of pleading. "Margaret can't go to the magistrate. You can see that. I'd planned to deal with her myself —send her far away—but that decision was taken from me when Scotland Yard turned up."

Cynthia nodded, her face wan. "I have a chum whose father is something in the Home Office. I could have a word. See what he can do."

She meant her friend Miss Townsend, whose father was prominent in the ministry that oversaw the police departments. I'd never been certain what he did, but apparently, Mr. Townsend was quite powerful.

"I would be grateful," Lord Babcock answered. "For now, Margaret, you should confine yourself to your bedchamber."

"You know *she* did it." Lady Margaret pointed once more to Lady Babcock, who sat in stoic perplexity. "If you search her chamber, you'll find the knife. <u>She</u> killed your son, because she's an evil, evil woman." Tears, true ones, streamed down Lady Margaret's cheeks. "I only want to marry Desmond. *To marry Desmond ...* "

Her knees buckled as she trailed off. Cynthia hurried to catch her before she fell, Mrs. Seabrook rushing in again with the smelling salts.

Before either could reach her, Lady Margaret came to life, struck out at Cynthia, and then lunged at me.

I gazed into the eyes of a young woman who'd never been denied anything, who thought she could do what she pleased to obtain what she wanted, even something as heinous as killing her own brother.

I brought up my arm to fend off her blows. Lady Margaret managed to strike me twice before Mrs. Seabrook seized her around the waist and dragged her from me.

Margaret turned to the housekeeper and sagged in her arms, relapsing into tears. "Help me, Seabrook. Make them leave me alone."

"There now," Mrs. Seabrook's voice went surprisingly soft as she gathered Lady Margaret to her as though she were a child. "There now. It will be all right."

I wasn't certain how it could be, but at Mrs. Seabrook's words, Lady Margaret quieted. Mrs. Seabrook held her for a moment, stroking her back in its ill-fitting frock, then eased Lady Margaret out of the room, a supporting arm around her.

Lord Babcock's face was like stone. Losing both of his children in the space of a day must be a terrible blow. I had a daughter of my own, one I'd see this afternoon. If anything happened to Grace, it would break me.

"Go," Lord Babcock said to me before I could form any words of compassion. "Leave my house, where you have caused so much trouble. Cynthia, take her, and do not return yourself. That goes for your tedious aunt and uncle as well."

"Of course," Lady Cynthia answered. She was polite

enough not to remind Lord Babcock she'd just offered to use her connections to lessen Lady Margaret's sentence. "Good afternoon, Lady Babcock, Miss Jordan." Cynthia nodded at them then ushered me to the door.

I sent a glance at Miss Jordan, who returned my look with a nod. The police probably would find the murder weapon in Lady Babcock's chamber, because Margaret, who'd been ensconced in that room most of yesterday afternoon, had the opportunity to hide it there. Miss Jordan, I surmised, would make certain the police knew Lady Babcock had nothing to do with that.

As Cynthia and I slid out, Lady Babcock rose and went to her husband. He remained stiff when she touched his arm and spoke quietly into his ear.

All at once, Lord Babcock transformed from the cold aristocrat to a father who'd never thought he'd have to face the things he had today. His mask dropped, and he turned to embrace his wife, his shoulders drooping.

I closed the door, and Cynthia and I moved quietly away.

When we left the house, Inspector McGregor, who had been waiting outside, gave Lady Cynthia a nod and me a more grudging one before he and Sergeant Scott approached the front door. Cynthia and I left them to it.

"Well, that was beastly," Cynthia declared as we trudged from Portman Square toward Oxford Street. A sudden wind struck us, as though trying to scour from us the sadness of the house we'd just departed.

"Yes," I agreed. "But if we had said nothing, Lady Margaret might not have stopped with Lord Alfred and Mrs. Morgan." I tried to feel high-minded about revealing her guilt, but I could not. I could only picture Lord Babcock collapsing in grief into his wife's arms.

Cynthia deflated. "I know. Ah, well, I'll be off to speak to Judith. Greet your little girl for me."

My heart lightened when I thought of Grace. She'd be waiting.

Cynthia and I parted, she heading to Upper Brook Street to visit Miss Townsend while I made my way toward the City and the house where my daughter dwelled.

As I strode along, the melancholy the house in Portman Square had settled on me began to ease, though it would leave its mark.

If Mrs. Bywater hadn't been the interfering busybody she was, I'd have only heard of the death of Lord Alfred in passing. I'd feel sorry for the family then return to my tasks, the event soon forgotten.

Then again, if Mrs. Bywater hadn't volunteered my services, Mrs. Morgan might be dead of too large a dose of morphine, and Lady Babcock might have been arrested for both murders. I'd done some good, I reminded myself. Also, for the first time in her life, Lady Margaret would have to answer for her misdeeds.

It would be a long time, however, before I forgot the cruel desperation in Lady Margaret's eyes and the acknowledgment on Lord Babcock's face that his choices in life had led, if indirectly, to the loss of both his children.

I drew a long breath as I walked, letting the spring breeze refresh me. It was a lesson, I decided, to balance love with responsibility, and to see that my daughter never had cause to despise or fear me. I would be as good to her as I possibly could, for now and for always.

My feet hurt by the time I reached Cheapside, as I'd been too distracted to seek an omnibus or a hansom. The ache receded as I turned to Clover Lane, where Grace lived with my dearest friends.

I felt a warmth at my side and started as Daniel fell into step with me and slid a firm hand through the crook of my arm.

I hadn't seen Daniel since he'd looked in on me early this morning to tell me he'd related all I'd told him to Inspector McGregor. The inspector had been most annoyed, of course, but he'd realized he had to release Cousin Desmond and had sourly sent the order.

I hadn't noticed Third Cousin Desmond rushing to Mount Street to assure Lady Margaret he was well. I wondered if he'd fled back to his home, wherever it was, to recover, and whether he'd already concluded what Lady Margaret had done.

"Your troubles are not allowed here," Daniel told me, scattering my thoughts. "The rest of the afternoon is for joy."

"Not joy," I quipped. "Grace."

Daniel's laughter rumbled, and with his strength beside me, I believed I could tackle anything.

My spirits lifted still more when Grace opened the door of the little house on Clover Lane and rushed out to me.

I caught my daughter in my arms, felt her kiss on my cheek, and absorbed her excited greeting. Daniel waited for us to finish our embrace, his eyes warm.

I was a woman blessed, I decided. I would savor this happiness for as long as I possibly could.

"That was a nice, squishy hug," Grace proclaimed when I at last released her. "Let us go inside, and you can give Aunt Joanna a squishy hug too."

Daniel's laughter boomed, lighting the overcast day. I clasped Grace by one hand, Daniel with the other, and together we rushed into the house, laughter and sweetness floating on the April wind.

The Necklace Affair

A Body in Berkeley Square

A Covent Garden Mystery

A Death in Norfolk

A Disappearance in Drury Lane

Murder in Grosvenor Square

The Thames River Murders

The Alexandria Affair

A Mystery at Carlton House

Murder in St. Giles

Death at Brighton Pavilion

The Custom House Murders

Murder in the Eternal City

A Darkness in Seven Dials

Leonidas the Gladiator Mysteries

(w/a Ashley Gardner)

Blood of a Gladiator

Blood Debts (novella)

A Gladiator's Tale

The Ring that Caesar Wore

Brother at Arms

ABOUT THE AUTHOR

New York Times, USA Today, and *Wall Street Journal* bestselling author Jennifer Ashley has more than 100 published novels and novellas in mystery, romance, historical fiction, and urban fantasy under the names Jennifer Ashley, Allyson James, and Ashley Gardner. Jennifer's books have been translated into more than a dozen languages and have earned starred reviews in *Publisher's Weekly* and *Booklist*. When she isn't writing, Jennifer enjoys playing music (guitar, piano, flute), reading, knitting, hiking, cooking, and building dollhouse miniatures.

More about Jennifer's books can be found at
http://www.jenniferashley.com
and
http://www.katholloway.com
To keep up to date on her new releases, join her newsletter here:
http://eepurl.com/47kLL